T0063372

A Garland for Aphrodite. Tales within a Tale from Cyprus by Sean Toner is a novel made up of a series of episodes with a common protagonist in all of them. Set on the island of Cyprus, the narrative traces the psychological journey of an English botanist, from *Freudenschaft* to inner restitution. Toner handles his narrative with subtlety and ties this to a profound understanding of the Cypriot landscape and the mythology of the island. This is a novel which will appeal to a wide variety of readers for its emotional depth of understanding and its restrained dramatic force.

Antony Johae: Associate Professor of English and Comparative Literature, author and poet

Sean Toner weaves a story from many short stories which he has carefully crafted to lead the reader on a journey, geographical and psychological, around the island of Cyprus. As he moves the action from Paphos and the Akamas to Kyrenia and Famagusta, the reader feels he has a camera on his shoulder, scanning the surrounding sea and countryside and panning in on the Cypriot characters that populate the book. This book is a literary tour de force which, I feel, could also become the inspiration for an excellent television series.

Robert Conlon: Former journalist and television regulator in the UK

Although, generically, *A Garland for Aphrodite* can be designated a Composite Novel, it may also be seen as a *Bildungsroman*, or a Novel of Education. It is the story of a man who is transformed by his encounters with an island's people, its visitors, its flora and fauna and the still present power of its myths.

Don Friend : Founder and CEO of SkySoftware.UK

A
Garland
for
Aphrodite

Tales within a tale from Cyprus

Sean Toner

For book orders, email orders@traffordpublishing.com.sg

Most Trafford Singapore titles are also available at major online book retailers.

Printed in Singapore.

ISBN: 978-1-4907-0305-3 (sc)
ISBN: 978-1-4907-0306-0 (hc)
ISBN: 978-1-4907-0307-7 (e)

Trafford rev. 01/27/2014

 www.traffordpublishing.com.sg

Singapore
toll-free: 800 101 2656 (Singapore)
Fax: 800 101 2656 (Singapore)

The author would like to dedicate this book to Vasiliki, Ben, Andrew and Vince who shared the years in Cyprus

Gratitude is due to the International Writers Workshop members who read and critiqued early versions. Special thanks go to Antony, Amanda, Harvey and Michael

Thankyou, too, to Kostas Tzelatis, the young film maker, cartoonist and illustrator who created the cover and the pencil drawings.

EPISODE 1

The botanist's day out

It was his third week in Cyprus and still the summer heat was warming the rich vineyards of the Akamas region, on the island's western flank. Cyprus could boast of all-year-round sunshine, but now, at the end of August, it was the most pleasant time of the year. In the taverna of Tremithousa, John Sampson had been nick-named the *votanologos*, the 'Flower-Man', as his Greek slowly improved and he was able to bring in and talk a little about specimens. He appeared there each evening about five for a beer or two before he went up the hill, usually about eight, to collate his articles and specimens and listen to the news on the BBC World Service.

It was a Wednesday and Wednesdays and Fridays were his days for putting on the boots and getting out into the National park. Today, Pappas, the village priest, had lent him his Peugeot pick-up, with a cursory warning about the brakes needing pumping. John had accepted gratefully. He was only too happy to have a vehicle with a suspension that could take the tracks through the Akamas Park region. In any case, he knew that regulations in that part of the world were not too stringent about brakes, lights and other safety features. So, he was growing to enjoy the risk element. Life was a risk. He'd risked something by coming to Cyprus in the first place, when he boarded that plane to Paphos last month, to fly away from the security of his regular, if somewhat constrictive, job.

He'd been subject to a sort of depression since his divorce because his inner confidence was in question. What had happened, he argued with himself, was no more his fault than it was Susan's. Yet there was this inexplicable sense of failure. He had failed; he who had never before failed an exam. Before this he had always passed the test. Had anyone attacked his theses, his academically stunning and avant-garde treatises which linked the geological rifts of the last twenty million years with the flourishing of hedgerow flowers in England, he would have been able to have fobbed them off, written a paper or two, retreated deep into the folds of academia. Now, marriage to the girl he had admired for her academic prowess had ended, feelings of hurt, feelings of absence, feelings of panic at the loss of the familiar had overtaken him.

After three pumps on the brakes, he managed to bring the Peugeot pick-up to a halt, deep in the heart of the National Park, as it had recently come to be known. The track ran out at that point, on a low elevation near the sea. Around him, on the ground, he noticed the skid tracks where the British Army vehicles had manoeuvred and turned after an exercise. He had been reading in 'The Cyprus Mail' about the controversy between the Cypriot authorities and the British forces, based at Episkopi, over the use of the Akamas as a shooting and exercise range.

John knew he had a good three quarter hour climb to scramble up to the high ridge which loomed above him. If any rare flowers grew at all in this region, the probability would be to find them in those high cliff tops, unreachable by most walkers and tourists.

As he pushed his way through the thick gorse, flecked here and there with Troodos rockcress, which populated the curving slopes above the beach, he could see, to his right, in the bay, the lapping shores of that ancient and most civilised of seas. He knew, from his recent reading on the history of Cyprus, that this was a sea of Homeric epic, a sea of Phoenicean trading adventure, a Crusader's sea, an Ottoman sea, a sea for some time associated with the British Empire. John had recently been able to witness, with his own eyes, how it had grown to be a tourist sea where all the main European societies came together, on the Mediterranean's most easterly island, to recharge their batteries every summer before re-engaging, come the autumn and winter, in their regular lives of political standoff and economic struggle, back on the European continental landmass.

The goat-track he eventually found led steeply up through tangled brushwood, dotted here and there with wild sage and irises and then, five minutes on, loose stones began to roll under his boots as pure rock took over from any discernible beaten track. Suddenly he was looking for hand-holds to pull himself up the steep wall that faced him. With his body stretched out against the toughened limestone, his cheek pressed against the smooth slabs of this spit that towered upward above the sea, John Sampson felt, for one moment, that he was back in undergraduate days when he would spend his weekends in the Lake District negotiating challenging rock faces and shale-filled gulleys. A rope would have helped here with the immediate difficulty of the sharp ascent. As he pulled with his fingers and pushed with toes, his trained nose took up the scent of the delicate 'Lady Slipper' flower. Although it was not the rarest species in Cyprus, it was one that his collection could not be without. It was endemic to European islands like Cyprus, much like the other ten he had, in his last three weeks here, managed to locate and label.

He found himself wondering about the goats that scrambled over these steep slopes. After all, they had been fashioned by evolution to keep their noses continuously close to the earth. Did they get this exhilarating feeling of recognition when the right smell overtook them? The feeling of expectancy of what might be over the mountain edge, like the shocking and abundant growth of a rare and beautiful plant, could provide an equally strong sensory experience for a scientist like himself.

He fancied that somehow, and no doubt mysteriously, the power of the ancient goddess of Cyprus extended to these high retreats as though her cult, which had dominated the whole Greek world for thousands of years, had never died, only receded to quieter places. It was as though she had removed her presence from the now crumbling temples and altars which surrounded Paphos and, he had to smile at his own imagery, gone into retirement in the remote reaches of the Akamas Peninsula.

A rush of adrenalin coursed through his veins as he scaled the short perpendicular section that distanced him from the top, as agilely as though he were indeed one of those mountain goats that he had been picturing. One more foothold—the rock held. One final pull up and the gush of air, as sea met the rocky outcrop.

A deep sense of satisfaction at having reached the top displayed itself in a flicker of humour, written on his face. Sampson, Professor Emeritus of Botany, (Oxon) playing the hunter looking for his quarry, ready to risk all, to surmount all obstacles, driven by instinct to find his prey. He felt so distant from his former Oxford don self, who would discuss with the Warden of Brasenose, at formal dinners, anything from the finer elements of aesthetics and William Blake's poetry to nuclear physics and politics. He scrambled up onto his feet and what hit his sweating face and torso, although too easily described, he knew, in simple scientific terms, as purely evaporation of sweat, was more than that. It was a breath of intoxication and power, as he reeled three hundred feet above the water, which altered the physical and psychological constants of his normal self. Just as his body temperature had dropped suddenly, so too, as he looked down to the sea, the familiar feeling of vertigo, which in recent years had haunted him, began to creep in.

An image, almost imperceptible, like a waking dream passed over his consciousness. He imagined for a fleeting second that he had, inadvertently, stumbled upon a place of special beauty, where the Goddess might lay herself down, her hair bedecked with 'Lady Slipper,' the scent of which, now in reality, filled his nostrils. He was, in his mind's eye, looking down and far to the Mediterranean. He could just descry the promontorial sands which were of another epoch—the landing points for the ancient kingdom of Amathus. The Eastern Mediterranean possessed a magic, very real and now very fearsome. It was an area attacked by many passing empire-builders but which had always retained its special status within, yet beyond, their power.

Back in reality the pungent aroma in the air increased his sense of vertigo, yet he remained shakily on his feet. Just as entering a forbidden place is a fearful experience, so fear of falling to earth, where perhaps his mind would not be in control,overtook him, and caused him to tremble. Then the fear became reality. He sank down helplessly to his knees. Through his fading vision, he could just make out the swooning drop that menaced him from a distance of only a few feet. For the strangest reasons, all his past passions and loves now returned-faces, contortions, anger, resentment, the making ups. He'd heard that, when people are dying, their past lives come up before them in no particular order. A sudden anguished pain grasped his chest and, although he knew it as a symptom of a panic attack, he'd had many since the divorce—each time it hit him he believed it could mean the end. His blood would race and his breathing would labour. Sometimes he passed out completely.

Time too seemed to take on new dimensions. The clock no longer proceeded in any ordered manner. The sun seemed to shut itself out and distort day, night and the corridors of years in some sort of Ouspenkian orgy. Where was yesterday? And greetings to two millennia from now. He was a child on his bicycle in another part of the planet, lost in a trance on a windy day, and then, suddenly, he imagined himself old, tired and ready to let go.

As the fear and disorientation left one mark and then created another, Sampson found himself coming round, aware only that a deep sensual yearning, like a young awakening, had replaced the panic. As his breathing regularised, he realised that the scent in the air was really alluring. There was an overwhelming feeling of the presence of the hauntingly beautiful.

The terror, that the arrhythmia had entailed, subsided and drained away from him. But, then, a rustling movement, of something or somebody, was coming up through the scrubland and bush from the sea. Just as suddenly, a deer-like creature, which he knew, from the pictures he had seen of it, to be a Cypriot *agrinon,* appeared and, frightened by the presence of a human, leapt up to the higher outcrop to the left. As the animal landed, all four feet were like those of two ballet dancers touching the ground, simultaneously melting into one stance. The beautiful beast stood for two long seconds, planted delicately on the small ledge as though posing for a picture or a painting. Its mouth and nostrils quivered because, with the botanist downwind, human scent brought fear to the wild deer-goat. Then, with one bold leap, it was on the ridge and galloping away.

Now fully recovered from his panic attack, Sampson got to his feet. A fair, strong but calming, wind led him along the cliff top. Goat markings were evident on the tracks but, to left and right of the path, untrodden vegetation bloomed freely. Here and there the tell-tale wisps of purple and lighter hues of blue told Sampson that the famous wild orchids of Akamas were hiding here, amongst their camouflage of heather and gorse. Perhaps 'it' was here, along this very path. 'It', for John Sampson, was *Epigogium Aphyllum,* known by the lay person as 'The Ghost Orchid.' Classified as very rare in Europe in general, John had surmised that the Akamas region had the conditions to harbour such a secretive flower, one that could live underground for many years until the perfect conditions presented themselves for it to show itself.

Now the vista opened up the sea-caves of Drepanum, perhaps a kilometre away to the East, their white chalky exteriors contrasting with the blue waters that lay around them and ran into them. It was a place where, in a flight of fancy, one could imagine the Goddess might cavort. *Where she was, it was*—of that he felt convinced. The certainty of it invaded his presence in a most unscientific way. The *agrinon,* that most exotic creature and cousin of the French moufflon, sought high places where humans, apart from a shepherd or two, might never walk. No large groups of humans meant no treading, no picking of the rare beauty. There was an odd sense of causality there. A Goddess would hide her island's adornments where normally only the wildest of beasts, like the *agrinon*, would venture.

A cool detachment descended upon him as he walked, and all thoughts of urban centres or great library sanctuaries, like the Bodleian at his own University, and all those intellectuals massaging their substantial egos, with publications that few ever read, faded into a world of self-mockery. In his thoughts, at that moment, there was only the living flower.

Ella, he heard himself speak in his bookish Greek—Come on, *Ella, Ella. Tora*—come, come to me now. The only reply was the tinkling of bells-melodic, completely part of the dreamlike sequence of events that had overtaken him that afternoon. "Goats" he thought. "A whole herd of them.!" And sure enough, as he was looking down to the olive plantations below, a somewhat wizened character, difficult to make out against the gnarled olive trees in the foreground of Sampson's vision, looked up grinning, beckoning to him to come down but to be careful of the steep descent.

"*Ella . . . Proseche ta petra . . .*"

Sampson descended quickly and came away from the view of the sea. He went over to greet the shepherd.

"*Iasu, ti kaneite*"

He was somewhat relieved to feel the presence and warmth of those simple animals, that appeared so much at home in their rocky surrounds, and was comforted by the broad smile the simple goat herder offered. He felt somehow closer to his quest because he had the Cypriot peasant's great bony hand shaking his own—so English by comparison.

Goat herders in the Akamas, Sampson guessed, did not get the opportunity to meet many people and the old man seemed only too happy to share his stories. Amazingly for such a peasant herdsman, he could project what he wanted to say using only a basic vocabulary of Greek, as he deliberately spoke slowly for the foreigner to understand. All the days of his grown life, it transpired, the Cypriot had pushed his herds up to the point where this outcrop met the sea. His wiry frame only highlighted the breadth and width of his vision. Yes, one time he had gone over to Kathikas village, ten miles from there, for a wedding. John gathered, from the Cypriot's dismissive laugh, that he thought of those village people as some sort of pompous asses.

"No. better to be your own man with your goats. I stay in my small hut about three miles from here and I would not swap it for anything."

The flower man had taken out his 'Rare flowers of the Eastern Mediterranean' and held out page forty four, now so well thumbed, in front of the man.

"Have you seen this small flower? Yes this one with with the white and purple flower? Looks like a . . . ?" Sampson paused, because he did not know the Greek word for a shroud. So he pulled a ghostly look and, holding his arms wide, took on the shape of a ghost.

He did not need to explain further. The posturing and photograph had sufficed.

"Yes that flower We locals always knew it was difficult to find. My father and my grandfather before him have seen it, but it is rare. Still,I can tell you, if you find it anywhere, it'll be in these few square miles between here and Drepanum and always near this lime rock and the sea."

Sampson had sensed he was in the right area. It had been there once. Was it still to be found? The Cypriot pushed his goats ahead quietly and, after a few hundred metres silent walk, introduced the stream that trickled back over the mountain edge and made a crystal pool. It was the clearest water imaginable. Sampson was aware that consecutive ice ages had locked in, over a billion years or so, two-thirds of the water supply on earth and the other surface liquid was simply recycled. Everything had been recycled but on the way some magnificent botanical specimens had been created, trodden on and died. To meet one beauty and not pick it up was something akin to the respect between a priest and a virgin. Man needed to help protect the fruits of the earth. The bulldozers were already busy digging up the surrounds of Paphos to build six more hotels. The Akamas, John knew, had just been declared a National Park but the act had been passed in the Nicosia Parliament by only a hairsbreadth, opposed by the large landowners and developers who had greedy eyes fixed in that direction.

The pool lay deep, quietly reflecting back distorted images of the two mens' heads.

"*Afto Eene*" said the shepherd. "This is our pool of Aphrodite."

Tourists, the flower man knew, flocked to another pool near Latchi, fed by a stream dripping from the Akamas heights, called 'Aphrodite's

Baths'. He mentioned it to his companion. The old man chuckled in answer:

"But I'm sure she's too shy to bathe where everyone goes—she's much more likely to be around here somewhere—*Eh-re-avtee ee Aphrodite eene thavmasia kopella*—She's quite some girl that Aphrodite!"

Looking again at his 'Rare flowers of the Eastern Mediterranean', Sampson remarked, beside the worn sketch of the flower, the soil and culture pedigree: *Epigogium Aphyllum*. Very rare in Europe—having no leaves as it does not depend on photosynthesis but rather on fungus that feeds its roots—growing underground for many years before surfacing beside or near wet areas., Sighted in 1928 by Williamson, near St Hilarion village, North Cyprus and 1976, Ord at Drepanum, Akamas.'

Walking around and about Aphrodite's 'private pool,' he amused himself thinking of her sunning what he imagined might be her beautiful upturned breasts by the pool, after bathing. Then picking the pretty little shoe flowers to adorn her hair. Later, walking back along the cliff surveying her empires, marine and terrestrial, calling wounded hearts back to what's natural.

The old goat herder had pointed out that the dearth of rain that year had left the pool very shallow, hardly able to breathe life into the normally lush vegetation surrounding it.

"Then echi auto to louloudi".

The shy ghost flower was not here this year, then. Rain was needed and there wouldn't be any for now. You could not expect any until November.

"Then perasi—It doesn't matter" said Sampson "I have time. I'll come back"

Ten minutes later the goats, familiar with their path, led the two men back on to the track where he'd parked the jeep.

"I'll come back" he reiterated . . . . shaking the big brown hand *"Kai evharisto!".*

As he pulled out of the track to head for the main coastal road to Polis, Sampson knew that the flower was, in a sense, secondary. It was the Goddess of Cyprus and her secret retreats he had to find first and, once located, to secure from her, by whichever means possible, her blessing in his quest.

EPISODE 2

A garland for Aphrodite

The village of Tremithousa was physically divided, by the single road running down the hill, into those who went to Akis and Soulla's place, known to support the right wing government and the church, and those who stared across from the 'drinks only' *cafeneion,* old boys who had supported communism, some as far back as the late fifties and the sixties. From behind their copies of *Neos Socialismos,* they were only able to smell and guess at the delicacies that Soulla laid out for her guests each evening.

John was normally to be found at Soulla's, where he was always recognizable by the battered Panama he wore and by his choice of table, in the corner of the forecourt. Politics had nothing to do with it. He just loved Soulla's food.

It was one of those balmy September evenings, that were so special to Cyprus, and the lamb chops were being prepared in the back kitchen. The smell of the oregano and lemon coating, magnified by the closed warmth of the clay oven they were cooked in, hinted at an extraordinarily tasty dish to come.

He had only been here five weeks or so and, since he was still taking stock of his surroundings, he always kept a map and a guide book on the chair beside him. Down below the village, situated as it was on the south western slopes of the Troodos range which descended majestically down to Paphos and the sea, the Mediterranean would have begun to brood under the full moon, as it was now rising. But, from the bottom of the hill, the view opened only to the west, to Coral Bay and the tiny village of Emba.

The street had taken on an air of expectancy, cloaked as it was in fresh nightfall and just out of view of the Polis road coming up from the town of *Pano,* or Upper, Paphos. There had been a good share of the *Englesi* who had made it to the taverna tonight, because Kokkos, the son of the village headman, quaintly called by the Turkish title, *Mukhtar,* had brought them up from the five star Annabelle Hotel in his mini bus, promising them that there would be an unusual spectacle this night which would involve Aphrodite herself. They had pushed him for more information but he had told them to be patient, for it would be a surprise. The group of tourists was just large enough for Soulla to handle comfortably, because, even she, who gained from the lucrative trade of feeding foreigners, did not want the village completely overrun with *Englesi* or any other outsiders.

Even as an 'outsider', John had been reminded so many times already about the prime position of honey in this village. Tremithousa honey was famed throughout the Mediterranean because of the wild thyme that grew in profusion at that altitude. Some of the better delicatessens in London now sported this variety. It was, therefore, no surprise to see Sotiris, chief bee-keeper, sitting, one door up, with *Pappas,* the priest, outside the once dark-blue, but now light sun-bleached door which a heavily scuffed wooden board marked as *kentro.* This was an unchallenged honour for Sotiris.

Tonight the locals had taken their seats a little earlier. According to Mariantha, Soulla's mother-in-law who ran the *kentro,* something special was going to happen, and a good sized group of *Englesi* visitors were being brought in. Mariantha was queen matron in Tremithousa and, amongst other functions, she acted as Postmistress. It was, therefore, for her knowledge of other peoples' business and forthcoming events in the district that she was most sought after. Yet it had been established, only one hour ago, by Mariantha herself, that, on this particular occasion, she could not be precise as to the source of information. She had heard from Giorgos, who worked in Paphos Town Hall, who in turn had said that he had heard it from Demetris, a trustworthy type who worked in the wine-press, that a procession would wind itself up from *Kato,* or Lower, Paphos, that it had something to with Aphrodite herself, Goddess of beauty, protectress of the island, and that Tremithousa would be the terminating point.

Just a few yards down from where the village priest and the Honey man were seated, the lanky frame of the man under the Panama, known to the locals as Ianni and sometimes going by his nick name, the *votanologos*, was positioned to one side of the taverna entrance. He was sipping on a bottle of *Keo* beer and, having put down the 'Blue Guide,' had begun leafing through his copy of 'Rare Flowers of the Mediterranean.' On the dog-eared inside cover, there was some latin on a yellowing sticker and a name in large print: **Ex Libris. John Sampson.** This same John Sampson, presently seated in *Taverna Tis Soulla,* had a clear view up the street of Tremithousa and could see that *Pappas* was busy discussing the possible outcome of the Aphrodite procession with Sotiris, and he could even interpret the gist of their conversation by the wide gesturing of the priest. If the procession did come by, he guessed the village priest was saying, he might have to disappear quickly and say a word or two against it in church on Sunday.

John was already aware that the archbishop, whose pastoral seat was at Kikkos monastery, thirty miles in to the Troodos range, had a reputation of being ultra conservative and probably would be the sort to frown on the manifestation of such pagan festivals. But in truth, even that renowned cleric, as possibly the most powerful man in Cyprus (everyone knew the Orthodox Church owned most of the island), had to be careful of antagonising the Goddess. She epitomised Cyprus. She had become the lifeblood of Cyprus. Where would the tourist trade be without her? They came in their millions from the cold, perhaps less emotional, countries of the North to find the warmth of the island of passion and love, of which Aphrodite was the patroness. She, and all her other aliases, the long line of goddesses of fertility, had, after all, been associated with the island since long before Homer had paid due homage to her in his epics nearly three thousand years before.

Pappas would be wondering, however, why there should be any celebration connected with the Goddess in this month of September. Normally she was honoured in Spring because of the obvious links she provided with fertility and because the annual flower festival, the *Anthestiria,* allowed the young girls to dress up in ancient Greek costume. They would dance the *Syrto,* each one of them desiring to be a handmaiden of Aphrodite and to revel in the festival which celebrated beauty and love. John heard the priest cough and address Sotiris in a slightly raised voice:

"Yes, I will definitely have to let the bishop know and he will not like it. *Ochi, Then tou th'aresei*"

Soulla and Akis had put most of the chairs and tables together to form a centrepiece in the stone-floor forecourt which opened on to the road. The result was a mish-mash of different sized tables, covered with one single blue and white tablecloth. Her group of English tourists were already whetting their appetites with freshly shelled peanuts, washed down with glasses of Othello red and St. Panteleimon white.

To Akis' loud call of *'Yannis, koumbare mou, ti kanis?'* John replied *'poli kala Akis, ki esi?'* His greeting was in slow broken Greek, although the brown eyes, which looked out from the weathered face under the rim of the hat, and his dark beard and moustache would have allowed him to pass for a local in most settings in Cyprus.

The English visitors, a homogenous group united by nationality and the bond of the blue and white tablecloth, were darting looks across at him, trying, no doubt. to make out more about this man who sat alone in the corner. Meanwhile he caught snippets of their conversation. The girl who, he had now gathered, worked for Channel Four Television and who had become, by strength of personality, the unofficial guide for the group which had travelled out with her from Leeds just two days ago, seemed particularly curious about him. Had she already noticed that, although he seemed very much a part of the scene, using even a little Greek with the owners, his mannerisms betrayed an English upbringing. For one thing, he was painfully aware that he was holding his knife and fork in a most correct manner, which bespoke a background which was definitely not Mediterranean.

He put down the knife and fork in order to get a better grip with his hands on his chunk of meat, a huge Cypriot portion of mutton which Akis had set before him a few minutes ago. The hat! Should he take it off? In his better moments he fancied it give him the air of the international traveller, a typical Somerset Maugham character. At worst, it seemed to him as though he was hiding under it. Hiding and retreating from a past that he did not now like to recall

The Channel 4 girl, whom the others were referring to as Margo, shook back her copious red hair and flashed her striking green eyes at him.

"Aphrodite's coming to the island tonight then? Aren't we the lucky ones! Should have rung my producer at Channel 4 and asked if I could film it."

He was able to place her accent as Yorkshire but couldn't be more precise than that. His ten years teaching undergraduates at the University had provided him with the ability to pick out most regional English accents. She had such a winning face, this one, and her statement urgently required some form of response, although his first inclination was not to reply at all but to fob her off with one of those mannered English smiles that meant 'keep your distance.' He was reminded of the encounter he had had, all those years back, when he'd first met his wife on a punting jaunt on the Isis behind Balliol College in Oxford. The memory made him wince inwardly. He tried to forget as he gave his reply.

"Oh, really? This is the first I've heard of it. Then, come to think of it, she often pops in to see us".

The Yorkshire lass laughed out loud. 'Leaves her face all over the place too, it seems. She appears on everything from petrol adverts to wine bottles!'

John had lifted the rim of his hat to wipe the sweat from his brow. September in Cyprus was still hot, even though the sweltering heat of July and August had subsided. As he made this gesture he thought that his answer to the girl was only half tongue-in-cheek for he had to admit to himself that, since his arrival last month, he had been too often made aware of *Aphrodite* here in moody Tremithousa. She, the temptress, the ancient Goddess, had often come to mind, not featureless and armless as she was depicted on the statues in museums around the world, but as she looked out from the labels of the fine young wines called after her, the undisputed mistress of the Paphos area with all her powers, physical and psychological, apparently very much intact. In his own restless sleeps, alcohol—induced and too light for peaceful slumber, she had wistfully crept out from the bottle labels to stare challengingly, but somehow captivatingly, at him.

The English tourists who had been listening to the short exchange between Margo, who had travelled out on the same plane with them, and the man in the corner, were temporarily. appeased. He spoke English. He must be just like themselves, come along to see what was afoot in Tremithousa tonight. Besides there were further distractions, in the form of new delicacies arriving on the table. Soulla swept around them delivering twin plates of courgettes that had been fried with onion and eggs, *colocassi* with pork chops flavoured with coriander and village wine, the pickled celery setting off a centre of globe artichokes. If there were any spaces on the laden table, they were now quickly filled with dishes of bulgar wheat and smooth natural yoghurt to accompany the meal.

John looked up from his plate, just in time to see *Pappas*, a fine looking man of about forty five, aware of the kudos which surrounded him as representative of the Orthodox Church, get up from his chair at Mariantha's. The priest strode quickly down the few meters to the taverna and turned into the arched recess which doubled as the forecourt and restaurant. He had, no doubt, witnessed the arrival of the visitors from his seat outside the post office and, after letting them down a glass or two, had decided it was time to make his formal entrance. First he made his way over to John.

"*Yiannis, inda pou kamnis?*" he asked in thick Paphitiki mountain dialect. Without waiting for an answer, for he could see, by the bottle count on the table, that the Englishman, now on his third *Keo*, was in good enough health, he swung his bearded head, the long hair tied in a bun behind, toward the assembled company.

"Hello, welcome to Tremithousa. I invite you for wine to enjoy us. Soulla, bring three or four bottles of the best. Make it Aphrodite. That'll be very good for tonight's celebrations."

Soulla, who had just placed two large carafes of *choriatiko* village wine on the table, nodded respectfully, turned on her heel and returned a minute or two later with the bottles and an opener. She positioned herself to the left of the priest and tried her hesitant English.

"This Pappas! Please drink for pleasuring our priest."

The girl from Channel 4 barely suppressed a grin at the choice of words.

John could see the evening was unfolding just like a mini theatre piece. Lights up. The actors were on stage. The dialogue was beginning to flow. All were waiting to see what surprises the finale would bring. And *Pappas*, he mused, knew what tourists wanted; cool liquid inducement to loosen up the tongue.

John Sampson knew that what would follow would be the usual Q and A interchange between host and guests. He was content to stay in the wings for now, but he found himself searching the face of the Channel 4 girl for another hint of that smile. Something within him, which had not been allowed to surface over the last traumatic five months, wanted her to look his direction again and to continue the conversation. Perhaps she would light him up again when he thought he had buried anticipation for ever. The bitter divorce had left his soul shrivelled, without faith, a non-believer in love or its stirrings.

Pappas did the introductions: "*Yiannis* is our flower man. He knows the names of all the many fine flowers in Cyprus. He is famous in your country. *Yiannis*, have a glass of good wine."

"But I have beer" said John. He felt slightly embarrassed that Pappas had exposed him like this so prematurely. He would have preferred to have let the information slip out slowly to those he thought might appreciate his profession. People didn't always like experts. Especially not from the overworked field of conservation when all they wanted to do was to plant a house and a garden in the best spot available. No, you needed to slowly gain respect for what you were trying to do in the minds of others, then nurture and cultivate an empathy for such a job as his.

In a sudden flight of fancy, he found himself thinking of Aphrodite, imagining the Goddess as she had been described by Homer, ushered in as the white tops broke their assault upon the shores of Cyprus. She might have picked a small flower, perhaps even a rare species of orchid or cyclamen, and vowed that she would for ever protect it. Now here he was, three thousand years after she had first been worshipped as protectress of the island and of love itself, seeking a discovery. Was it these same rare floral specimens, he wondered, or a new self that he really wished to discover. Perhaps one quest would lead to the other.

Suddenly he was aware of the red-head looking over, the broad smile still playing on her lips and his question slipped out.

"Do they ever show the *Akamas* flowers on Channel 4? There are some very rare species of orchid and other flowers and, you know, even one or two that are endemic, belonging only to this island."

"Oh yes." she replied enthusiastically. "As a matter of fact, I am a TV researcher and I am doing some early research right now and into next week for a programme called 'Forgotten Treasures of Europe.' One episode will be about the environment and I've already been informed about the rare flowers that grow in this region. I expect they'll slot it in at midnight on Wednesdays. The violence and the sex take precedence at the prime time, of course."

She was a girl with promising wit, he thought. The fact that she could mock the media in this fashion pleased the somewhat cynical Oxford don which was his *alter ego*.

Akis brought in *sheftalia* and *souvlaki* on a large plate. The aroma of lemon and the thyme which had been thrown on the hot wood chips as the spicy sausage meat had cooked, enhanced its smoky flavour. Akis showed every one just how good it was by picking up two large, spiced, sausages with his fingers, dropping them into his mouth, then quickly washing them down with a good glug from a half-bottle of brandy. No delicate English manners there, thought John.

The general conversation lapsed, as everyone at table did justice to the fine Cypriot cuisine in front of them. People enjoyed their food more in unique settings like this. John knew that the rare flowers too had a unique setting. Their survival had required the pillow lavas and the metabasalts that volcanic eruptions had brought from the shores of Egypt to Cyprus at least ten million years ago. These, in turn, had been topped by sandstone and limestone formations that allowed for easy water migration, hence sating the thirst of flowers that existed nowhere else on earth. Then *she* had arrived, a straif who had wandered through a thousand Greek islands and along the southern coast of Turkey, flaunting herself on every inlet, led on by fate to arrive at the shores of Paphos. She'd taken up their cause, the cause of the forgotten flowers, protecting them from man's desire to tread them down, divert their water sources and destroy them.

Down from the top of the village street where the gamblers played, sometimes for the highest stakes, their houses, their fields, even their wives, came the first signs that Aphrodite might be near. The noise of clapping, shouting and whistling had reached the ears of those in the *kafenion* which afforded a better uphill view than did the taverna. The *mukhtar,* in his capacity of village head man, was first, from the group of aging *kommunistes* that assembled there each evening, to rise from his chair. He hobbled out into the street on his one good leg. The other had been crushed twenty years before by the red tractor, which was even now parked on the corner awaiting him.

As he looked up the street, John heard what sounded like a drum, almost drowned by the excited voices of the card playing gamblers. One large red-faced Englishwoman, still chewing on a piece of souvlaki, got up from Soulla's table and walked out into the street.

"There is quite a commotion goin' on up the street!" she cried.

"*Erkete*" announced the *mukhtar*, formally from over the road, for he had a clearer view of the approaching procession.

Soulla ran out and, in her excitement, dropped the tempting stuffed green peppers onto the cobbles of the courtyard.

"Now coming . . . now coming!" shouted Soulla, offering a rough translation of what the *mukhtar* had just said. Suddenly, all the others were on their feet and pushing to get a view.

John, normally one to sit back calmly until he had assessed a situation, was overcome with curiosity too. Suddenly, he found himself helping Margo to set up what looked like a medium-sized but professional video recorder, ensuring that a battery pack was securely lodged into the back of the machine and quickly popping the tripod where it would sit safely between the broken cobble stones.

"I hope the power will not run out now!" she shouted over the bustle and noise around her. "I'm not sure what's happening but I must get whatever it is on camera."

John felt her excitement as one of her breasts brushed his arm. As it's softness touched him, the skeletal muscles around his neck contracted and produced a cold shiver. He was not sure whether such a physical response was a manifestation of pleasure or embarrassment. After all, he mused, for nearly six months he had lived the life of a celibate.

Then the mystery of that night's visitor to Tremithousa was swept away, as the drummer, accompanied by a man playing the *kithara*, rounded the curve in the road just above Marianthi's makeshift Post Office. They were followed by a motley crowd of people who seemed to be leading and pulling something, some tugging at a rope, others swishing small branches. Soulla drew in her breath and, lifting her arms in the air delightedly, explained the scene to her somewhat puzzled customers.

"Ah, it's Aphrodite the old donkey. She come back after too many years! She finish now from the Wine Press in the town." Soulla, long suffering wife of the domineering Akis who preferred to spend his evenings with Filippina exotic dancers at the Bonanzo Bar at Coral Bay, was suddenly transformed, her smile infectious.

The Channel 4 girl felt positively charged as she looked over at Soulla. She quickly turned the camera towards her to capture this poignant moment of joy.

"This is great" the Yorkshire lass exclaimed. "I can't believe I'm really here to witness this. What a turn up for the books. A donkey!"

The *Pappas* looked very definitely relieved that now he could report only a very innocent event in his next letter to the archbishop.

Aphrodite came nearer and the old character presently holding her bridle, drunk with the double excitement of driving the beauty home and of having probably emptied more than one bottle of *koniaki* at various stages on the way, had already approached the stage of staggering. Indeed, it seemed to John that the donkey was leading him.

The English tourists made their way back to the table, many faces displaying a sort of quizzical expression. It hadn't been quite what they were waiting for but, in a way, it had turned out better than expected. It had the makings of a good anecdote; one to tell the neighbours in Leeds over the holiday snapshots. Fancy Aphrodite turning out to be a donkey! The botanist, too, was about to retire to his corner and order another bottle of *Keo* beer, in celebration, when he noticed Aphrodite's crown. Garlanded with unusual species of Cyprus flowers, the celebratory wreath, which he knew they called *stefani* in Cypriot, hung between the two high-cocked ears.

Aphrodite gave one glance over to the tables. The poor old girl, thought John, having done many a year pulling the grape carts at the wine press down in Kato Paphos, had seen similar faces, human, unforgiving, sometimes intolerant of her needs.

"Get a shot of those flowers if you can!"

John was urging the Yorkshire girl to turn the lens on the donkey's head. Just in time too, for Aphrodite was about to round the corner where the road led off to the fields behind the *kafeneon*. Would the camera catch, he wondered, the deep satisfaction in the animal's eye as she caught the smell of the prickly pear field beyond. Probably only two kinds of people, the professional such as himself and the intuitive peasant of the Paphos villages, could know what a delicacy that spiky fruit was for the equine species.

The botanist, approaching through the night shadows to stroke her head, smelt the sharp pungency of her used body mixed with the sweet aroma of what he thought must be mountain orchids.

Demetri, one-time owner, now to be her caretaker in her retirement, came out to the corner, patted her tenderly on her neck and led her home.

John took his seat. This time, Margo was beside him at the corner table. He was to join her in a glass of the white wine.

"Hey, any chance we could go looking for some forgotten treasure together soon?" asked Margo

A small hesitation. Then: "Don't see why not. I'm going Kathikas way on Tuesday, if you want!"

"Lets drink to that!" she replied.

They raised the glasses high and John gave the Greek salute of health. "*Yamas!*"

"*Yamas!*" she repeated, heartily and without hesitation.

EPISODE 3

Tremithousa bus

From his vantage point, down the single road that ran through the village, John could make out the English family, who lived next to Tremithousa's main gambling den, hurrying out of the house. But Andreas, the driver, in true Cypriot fashion, would not be thinking of how late he was running; that was for sure. The boys hurrying out of the door, flat pitta bread sandwiches in hand, had incongruously red-blazered outfits with ties to match, upon which a sombre owl stared out as if in warning, should anyone fail to respect the insignia of British International Education.

They were on their way to the English International School, equally incongruously housed in an old Greek military caserne in Upper-Paphos. When the bus did eventually appear at the brow of the hill, John's keen eyesight picked out the details on the front roller display. Andreas had, that morning, changed the destination on the roller from Blackpool to Margate. The one-time excursion coach had been shipped out from England in the early seventies and, thirty odd years later, was still serving the mountain community beyond and above Paphos.

The old crock's bright pink exterior had led the English boys to divulge to John their nick-name for it: 'The Pink Panther'. Inside were patched brown cloth seats and wooden facia which bespoke better times when it had picked up in sedate towns such as Tunbridge Wells and Lewis and swept off happy families to the Kent beaches for the day. Now there were the signs of advanced aging. The back window allowed plenty of ventilation to enter straight on to the necks of the two older English boys who took up the long back seat. This was not because the windows of the early 1970s had been designed to fulfill this function. No, the Margate bus had no pane in the back window at present. Nobody really wished to complain, in case the fare went up from the one shilling—or a few cents if you carried the new euro—that it had cost for the last five or so years. Moreover, because it was still hot in Cyprus in early October, people were very glad of the extra circulation. Direct sunlight was blocked at the rear of the bus by a pair of tattered blue curtains which flapped incessantly, thereby creating the effect of a noisy fan.

By the time the Panther arrived at John's stop, the last of the boys was still fumbling for his *ena shillinga.*, the one with the bird on, the equivalent to a twenty cent coin. The youngest boy had taken up co-driver position right up beside Andreas and, pleased as punch at occupying this important position, the five-year-old leaned over to move the steering wheel. The driver tried out the boy's Greek.

"Iasu, re Vinkentio. Pos pai?"

Vincent, now renamed *Vinkentio* (a most ungreek name, thought John), was quick with his greeting.

"En taxi Andreas, ke see".

The boy's fluency, and the thick tones of Paphos dialect he used, brought a smile to the lips of the driver, as he pulled at the long loping gear lever and scratched it into first.

Moving off down the hill to collect the other regulars, the first house they passed was the gambling establishment. At this early hour in the day no sign, except some stubbed cigarettes and empty cognaki bottles lying outside the front door, gave witness to the tension engendered around the games tables the night before, when, perhaps out of money, or deeply in debt, men had put up the stakes. In a Cypriot poker game, houses, dowries, daughters and even wives were at risk: they were all valid currency. Past the bee-hives from where Tremithousa honey, pride of the Paphos region, emanated, past the black pig being fattened up for the Paschal activities.

The Botanist mounted the high bus steps every Monday and Thursday. Today was Monday—one of the days when Sampson gave Biology lessons at the International School. Naturally he always leaned the lessons towards Botany and today he was to take the third year out to the Drepanum Caves. Hence he felt a spring in his step as he moved forward to pay his 20 cents, nodding to his English colleague from the French Department, the one with the three boys., who sat with his Greek wife behind the driver.

He took his seat behind them waiting for the eccentric Kyria Loula to push over by the window. No sooner had she done so than she began her usual long and speedily executed monologue, which involved the village priest and how he had rescued a donkey that had fallen off the back of a pickup truck. She spoke to no one in particular and, every now and then, giggled uncontrollably at some private joke. She travelled on the bus every day, down to a day care centre in the town and every day she recited the same disjointed story. Sampson, getting on almost last, midway down the hill, usually had the pleasure of sitting beside her. She had one other eccentricity which was stealing clothes from the washing lines and hoarding them in an outhouse. This became a little embarrassing for the priest (he who centred in her story) when one day she stole three pairs of his long johns. The priest mentioned the incident in a sermon on honesty and thereafter the story became the subject of many ribald jokes in the taverna.

The old excursion bus pulled into the tight corner which harboured the Communist *cafeneion* and above which, from the eaves, a flock of pigeons took flight every time a vehicle rounded the corner. When the birds left, the village *kentro* would fall doubly silent, no pigeons flapping, no sound of an engine. The lane they took here was narrow and led to a solitary stone house which stood shaded by a large carob tree. In the field to one side, a rusty iron hospital bed sat under an olive tree where Kyria Pantelides snoozed with her sister every afternoon at siesta time. Now, she was attempting to climb up the steps towards the driver's ticket roll. Sampson had heard tell she was a hundred and thirteen years old. Bent double almost and unable to see, except at the closest of quarters, you could certainly believe she was very old; but a hundred and thirteen? Could anyone reach that age?

"Yes, she really is," her grandson, who looked all of sixty five, had told him one night over a beer at Soulla's. "She takes her pension down to the bank every Monday and that Artemio, the gambler who happens to be a poor gambler and also happens to have his name on the account, since her daughter was his godmother, has it all blown by Tuesday night." Then the grandson had crossed himself and murmured *"Panayia mou!"* in an ostentatious cry of desperation to the Virgin Mary.

Now she had finally reached the first step, but time this morning, Sampson thought, was on her side, not on that of the teachers at the International School. In twenty five minutes time, the Headmaster,

Michael George, would be standing at the gate beside the British ex-Air Vice-Marshall, recently appointed as Chairman of the Governors to give the appearance of high attachment. They would be checking teachers. Not so bad for him. They were glad of his name, Oxford don—well known botanist and so on-but for his other colleagues, who he knew were paid a pittance and who were treated with much condescension, it would be different. How glad he was, in all his experience of academia, that he had not ended up as a schoolmaster.

"Someone get out through the back door and give her a shove up!" Andreas yelled out, now somewhat impatiently, although this was a ritual he endured every Monday. One stout middle aged lady who was often to be seen washing the steps of the church, a stalwart of the parish, alighted from the back door and, with great aplomb, physically lifted the aged bundle onto step two. Andreas waved the fumbling for the twenty cent piece aside. No one would argue that she should not travel free at her age.

As the bus set off up the hill around the graveyard, which curiously crowned the rubbish tip area, Sampson reflected as in a reverie. Two months and a week here now, in this country where some people indeed grew very old. Others, he had heard tell, spent all their savings on the villa in the mountain only to be cut off one day on the treacherous mountain passes or had fallen seriously ill before they had time to enjoy their new surroundings. They had all fallen victim to the old myth-maker, the mistress of Paphos, the Goddess of Love, who lifted the sights of those who had been blown in Odysseus—like onto those shores. She brought them up on high, filled their ears with the rush of the east wind that came off the Mediterranean to cool the height of the Akamas and to dance the waves in to the sea-caves of Drepanum. The smell of the flowers of Cyprus intoxicated such exiles, as she used them like a perfume to lure. She had been around Cyprus for a very long time; from those early days when God had been a woman; her kind of woman.

The bus had now reached the next village of *Mesachorio*. Each day the Pink Panther made a long figure eight through the Paphos villages, before it steamed down the hill to Upper Paphos and the Caserne school. Andreas, the driver, was now in his own village and all the passengers were held at ransom. A coffee with his *koumbaros*, passed through the driver's window, would pay the price of moving on. *Koumbaros* was 'best man' but, in Cyprus, just about everyone carried this grand title, because all the village turned out for a wedding and for the small price of pinning of ten pounds on the bride you became *koumbaros*. Hence, everyone, including Sampson himself who had attended five weddings already, was addressed as *re koumbare* in conversation.

Five valuable minutes later, with the coffee finished and a few bags of groceries that Andreas had brought up from the early morning vegetable market passed out to his sister-in-law, the driver attempted to start up the old machine. A full bus prayed as the key turned once, twice and three times, without success. Andreas finally jumped out and, with two turns of the crank handle, the bus spluttered into life.

By this time the French teacher and his wife were anxiously looking at their watches, even practicing certain French *explosifs*, as they realized that once again they were going to be late. It was now just a question of how late. Being British meant being on time. Sampson,however, had refused, after his first month in Cyprus, to worry about such trivia as checking the time. He didn't even wear a watch any more. The Cypriots did not worry about keeping a close eye on the time, so why should he? The daily events that interspersed village life were timed by the sun or the kind of heat or coolness that permeated the air or by a bird's call. Ironically enough, he thought as he noticed Andreas' wry smile in the driving mirror, many things were timed by the arrival or departure of the bus. The bus was all things to the village. It carried the mail to and fro and people to work and back and it was a means of transport that was communal. Many left their cars behind just to feel a part of the community. Andreas was aware of his power as driver of the community vehicle and often liked to display a brinkmanship, which involved starting off slowly on his round of the villages, then driving like a bat out of hell down the last stretch to make up on time.

"God help us!" Sampson exclaimed loudly as Andreas, now charging downhill with the full weight of the bus behind him, raced to overtake a car, almost kissing the body of another of the mountain bus specials coming the other way. The road that dropped so steeply from Tsada, on the heights above, down to Pano-Paphos was indeed a death-trap. Lorries, John read every day in the paper, lost their brakes and careered out of control. The road itself had been built for minis which all the tourists had hired in the sixties and seventies and even into the eighties. Now the greater load of transport, as Paphos grew into the new millenium, could not be supported.

Just one more turn off—for the last village on the itinerary. Then, Sampson reflected, we'll be on the last stretch. School Assembly must have already started and what a difficult village this Stroumbi was to get back out of! Once they reached the market *kentro,* it was the end of the road. This necessitated a hair raising reverse movement round the church. Andreas, he had heard, took great delight in getting as near as possible to the village church. The priest there had favoured one of his own extended family over Andreas' uncle in a dispute over a *strema,* a thousand square metres of land. Delight lit up his eyes as he brought the pink bus to within half an inch of the corner of the church, all the women blessing themselves in case he should disturb the house of God.

This ritual over, the bus returned to the main road and soon it had pulled up outside the school gates, freshly painted, for this was now the fourth year in the life of the Paphos International School. Having been a military caserne once, it naturally looked a little foreboding. Right now, however, it looked even more forbidding, as Air Vice Marshall, John Whiteman, and Headmaster, Michael George, tapped their feet and scowled as the French Teacher, complete with wife and children, filed miserably by. Sampson proffered a "good morning" but did not get one back. Assembly had apparently not started yet, since there were not enough staff present to make it feasible.

"Oh John", Mr George called back "your bus is waiting for you—the children are all aboard for the Drepanum trip."

"They can wait a minute or two," John muttered to himself then, raising his voice, added: "Won't be a minute, just get my notes from the staffroom".

"Yes John and could you possibly get here a little earlier" added the Air Vice Marshall. John did not reply. Excuses sounded so schoolboyish.

Two minutes later, he was on the second bus, a sparkling new vehicle, which had been hired from the Scandinavian Tourism agents in Pano Paphos. He was greeted with great cheers by the assembled third year. He was very popular with them. After all, he tried to make his subject come alive and they did not see so much of him, in one week, as they did other teachers.

He was just about to rush up and down checking names and giving out the handouts he had prepared, when he stopped short and sank into a double seat. "Remember your adage" he said to himself "and think as the Cypriots do". He adjusted the straw panama which was beginning to show signs of wear after two months in the heat and many a walk through the thick brushwood up on Akamas heights.

He took out his 'Flowers of the Eastern Mediterranean' and found the section on Drepanum.

'One of the most beautiful spots in Cyprus,' it stated, 'where sea arches and sea caves have been fashioned out of the chalky limestone'. He stopped. Loulakis had come up, staring rather sourly at him.

"What's this place like then, sir?"

He didn't feel like really getting involved in explanations with Loulakis—who would normally keep you answering questions for an hour.

The choking noise of the bus trying to start made him rethink his answer. The new bus coughed and then died. The humidity that ran over into autumn took its toll on batteries and automatic starting systems in Paphos. He knew that the irony was there was no cranking system as backup on these new buses. Maybe this was an omen, he thought, that Paphos felt more comfortable with the old and familiar.

He smiled at the boy who had asked the question and answered him:

"We'll see when we get there shall we, Loulakis? Meanwhile can you go in and tell the headmaster that the bus won't start. I suggest he call up *Paphites,* the company that runs the *Epiarche* public bus service and ask for one of the old reliable ones."

Under cover of darkness

As John Sampson drove his newly acquired car, an old but solid white Volvo Amazon, out of the village of Tremithousa, to his left row upon row of the famous bee hives and to his right thick clumps of lemon groves, he convinced himself that now he felt a little more settled into the sleepy routine of his mountain abode. He had been quickly accepted into the pattern of daily life here and he knew he could not have been better positioned with the Akamas Peninsula, and the rare wild flowers that he needed to locate and label, only fifteen miles away

Since he'd been asked to give talks on the Akamas region at the local International School and to teach some Biology to the seniors, he had also begun to feel part of a wider community. He'd needed the social links more than anything else. It was part of what he imagined might be a slow healing process, that he had entered into as soon as he had arrived on those shores. He couldn't, after all, abandon himself entirely to what he imagined were the whims of Aphrodite, whose spectre haunted his fitful sleeps on a nightly basis. So he'd begun teaching two mornings a week.

Then Mrs. Dolly, deputy headmistress of the Paphos International School, had invited him over for socials.

"Now you're a staff member, John, make sure you get over to see us. We have card games, every Saturday afternoon, over at our villa."

This particular Saturday afternoon, the exterior of the Dollys' white washed villa in Marathounda village looked much the same as on the other two days the botanist had visited. Now, as at those times, the Pakistani jasmine, lining the path of Albanian stone that traversed the tidy

English lawns, remained folded, ready to release its intoxicating aroma as soon as night would come. The bougainvillea leant luxuriantly against the trellis which led up to where the vines provided shade to the door.

Today, however, John noticed immediately that there were no cars in the drive except one and it had the ominous sign of *ASTYNOMIA* printed in gold letters on to the blue background. What were the police doing here? A parking fine to collect? They sometimes came for that. There existed here a local door-to-door police service. The *Englesi* were quite a good source for parking and speeding fines which helped to fill up the coffers of the municipality.

He was on the point of ringing the bell for a second time when the Greek Cypriot policeman, hat in hand, rounded the corner from the back garden area.

"*Yiasou, kyrie . . . Ti thelete?*"

Sampson would have told him immediately why he had come, had he not felt the deadening sensation in the pit of his stomach that temporarily froze all response. Something was wrong. No cars belonging to the couple. A policeman circling the garden and house. An inspector followed, making his appearance from the side-door of the house. So they had been inside . . .

He tried his still hesitant Greek:

"*Pou eine* the Dollys? *Eime* invited!"

Speaking in this hybrid language, half Greek half English, was something John was becoming quite used to. It was nothing strange in Cyprus where, because of English colonial influence, many Cypriots spoke dialect Greek mixed with chunks of English. They had sisters, brothers, cousins living in London and the main UK cities. The connections were strong, especially in this Paphos area which had been now, for thirty years or so, the new resort for retired and semi-retired English people. Many of these had moved after the Turks had invaded the Northern sector in 1974, their army occupying Kyrenia, the former "darling" resort of the British.

The Inspector spoke in thickly accented but clear English:

"Sir, you have not heard? Mrs. Dolly is missing now for two days over the half term period. Her 'usband has reported this yesterday."

That's odd, thought Sampson, as he returned to his car. Celia would never go anywhere without notifying people and if Ray didn't know where she was, who did?

On the route to Limassol from Paphos, the old road, twenty miles out of Paphos, traces the edge of the cliff-tops. One of the most dangerous routes anywhere in Cyprus, Sampson had many times thought. One dreamy moment of inattention and you had the long drop in to the Mediterranean which, because of its very limited tidal action, always waited, in more or less the same position, to drink up what unexpectedly came out of the other 'blue'. Pursue the twisting cliff road beyond Kouklia for five minutes or so then you're racing down a straight and Aphrodite's Rock, also known as *Petra Tou Romiou,* is clearly visible. At night, if there was a moon, it was a hauntingly beautiful sight and the placid sea had often lured him as he had returned from giving a weekend lecture in Larnaca or from visits to the Art Museums in the capital, Nicosia. He'd parked up many a time, found his way down a pathway lit only by the moon and gone into the sea. He'd allowed his body to be massaged in the warm waters that had not yet cooled from the day's heat; climbed up on the rock and lay, as in the dream portrayals of certain Persian painters, for a good hour or so, dark blue visions warming his body with light.

Just on the other side of the small bay where Sampson was wont to go and in the direction of Paphos, were beaches too rocky for the tourists, the descent too steep from the road.

About fifty metres up the craggy hill side, away from the little bit of even sand you could find there, a Cyprus fox had just left his den one balmy night in October. Since darkness had long since fallen, the hunters would not be out and yet the moon would afford him tonight a perfect scavenging trip. He would start out with a quick trot over to the picnic spot which lay round the bay. The fox manoeuvered his scrawny body through the delves between the rocks. Had you been able to watch from the road above that night, so perfectly camouflaged was he that only a whisper of a shadow would have been distinguishable, as he darted here and there nosing in every crack and cranny.

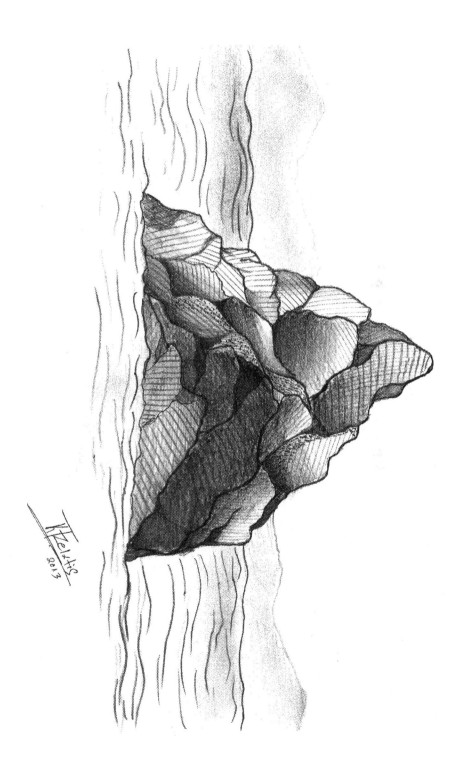

Baffled by the disappearance and even more by the ensuing silence on the part of the Police which had now endured into the third day, the botanist had arrived at the McKenzie house up in Tsada. They had already heard. But Celia was like clockwork; she was just incapable of disappearing without giving warning. Then, as they sat sipping cognac on the veranda which looked out and down to Paphos, the eye passing Marathounda on the descent, the light of a car, coming up the dirt track from below, came into view. Half a minute later the old Austin Five was in front of the house. The George family jumped out and Michael, the Senior Head Master, had no sooner reached the concrete step leading on to the veranda when he was asking:

"Have you heard about Celia?"

Discussion followed. She'd been under a fair amount of strain, what with the outgoings not matching up with the fees intake. It had all come to light in the accountant's report last week. Michael had been feeling the strain too but he'd felt certain the banks would help out until he had the boarding school section built. Boarding schools in Cyprus meant good business.

"Look, she probably needed a little peace and quiet for a few days, Ray. Stay calm, she'll be back when she's sorted herself out". Something like that you could imagine their British friends saying to Celia's husband. Sampson, however, looked out onto that large pond of the Mediterranean and he drew in his breath. If she had cracked up, where could she have gone? None of her closest friends had heard a word from her.

From the bay of Paphos he allowed his eyes to sweep up through the glittering lights which announced the position of the town, once a city, the ancient focus of the worship of the Goddess of Beauty and Fertility. Then his gaze moved to the right taking in the foothills of Troodos, a small pocket of light here and there indicating a village, where he was sure folk would gather in the taverna or the church to give each other encouragement when the dark mantle of night fell. He'd felt the ethereal strangeness of this Paphos countryside from the first day he had arrived there. He'd come looking for the kind of escape and the peace projected on the travel brochures. Although the sabbatical year, coming when it did, had been god-sent, it had only taken three months for him to learn that the island's ancient goddess, Aphrodite, was in charge here. In her effort to establish her reputation with him she was giving him a roller-coaster of a ride.

"Anything could have happened" he heard himself say out loud. No sooner had he uttered the words than he physically felt the shudder, like a cold electrical impulse, that ran up the spine into the nape of his neck and seemed to want to transfer itself into Mc Kenzie seated beside him.

The Cyprus fox, slighter in stature than its European cousin, less red in colour than tawny brown, was classified as an endangered species. Cypriots hunted everything: shot everything on sight. Saturday evenings were favourite with them and men crawled home late with rabbits and birds hanging off their gun-belts and a stomach lined with cognac. Hunting was a social affair for the Cypriot male and often ended up with drinks and animated conversation in the *cafeneion*. Way back in 1956, the British government of the then 'protectorate' had had to starkly control the shooting of the wild *Agrino*-half deer, half goat—a cousin of the French Moufflon. Cypriots did not think of the niceties of preserving species. They shot them for their tender meat. There had been only about thirty left anywhere in the world. Areas protected by barbed wire were set up at Stavros Tis Psokkas and other high places in the Troodos Range which were difficult to access. Slowly their numbers had grown.

The tawny fox was not similarly protected but, tonight, he felt nature was on his side as he moved nimbly over the rocky slopes near Aphrodite's rock. The large moon afforded him night vision. The sweet breeze blowing off the sea brought scents up to him from the beach. All he would have to do would be to skirt the upper edge of the rocky beach area where he did not expect to find anything special. Humans didn't go there—no sandwiches and half eaten chicken legs there—but round at beach two there should be some good pickings. Earlier that evening there had been the lights retreating as the picnickers had gone. He sensed then that there was no danger in the area. His luck, he felt certain, was in. But just as he was crossing one track that the foresters and beach clearance people used only when the sun was up, he saw the lights facing down to the beach. From the same point above him he heard the loud noise emitting from behind the lights. His bristles came out with fear. For the moment he would have to give up. Rounding on his back paws, he made off for his den, his hunger unabated.

The group members were brought out of their classes, the botanist from a slide-show where he had been showing those beautiful rare Akamas specimens, Mc Kenzie from the biology lab where he'd been dealing with red blood corpuscles: all into Michael George's cramped Headmaster's study to meet the detectives. The junior school teachers had already gathered there.

Kyrios Skourides began: "Ladies and gentleman we have to announce that Mr. Ray Dolly was arrested this morning. Traces of blood have been found in the house and in his Pajero".

"Good Lord! Does that mean he murdered her?" Mrs. Dolly's deputy's concern showed. All faces were white with shock.

"We can't talk about a murder until we have a body," replied the stony-faced detective.

The Cyprus fox, even hungrier, for he was not a day-time wanderer, had come out of his den the following evening. He had skirted the stony beach till a scent had come to his nose carried on the inland breeze up from the beach near that sandy area above which the human manifestation had come the previous evening. A smell had caught his attention. It seemed to say 'human' and 'human', without noise and without lights, seemed to say 'scavenge'. He changed direction, went towards the sea, placed his long nose into the sand and started digging.

They were all gathered in front of the bungalow in Tremithousa which Sampson had rented for the year, sipping Aphrodite white and red Othello. Even these light young wines could not keep the despondency away. The police had not said anything further for two days. There was still no sign of a body, although all of Cyprus was looking for it.

"Such a close couple—it's really unbelievable," said one.

"I saw them at the school production," another joined in. "She directed it so well, her children were all wonderful. She was so proud. He was on the lights and I saw her turn to him and the closeness in their looks when the play was over and the clapping had begun".

Sampson felt the tight clamminess which had been strangling the coastal area of western Cyprus for the past few days. The weather forecast was now showing on the portable TV which had been brought out and stationed on a table on the verandah. It threatened more humidity; unusual for late October, as everyone was saying. Something must break, the weather or the tension or both. He poured himself and McKenzie and his wife a long schooner glass each of Duc de Nicosie champagne. Local champagne was very affordable at three euros a bottle. Two ice-cubes fizzed and frothed the pinkish liquid to the surface of the glasses.

Then, the forecast over, the familiar music of the six o' clock news brought everyone's attention to the screen. Six days she had been missing and for six days the staff of the Paphos International School had met in each others' houses, trying to answer impossible questions, comforting one another, brought together, all ten of them, by a knowledge that all was not right. Blood had been found. Ray had been arrested but no-one had got to see him. Rumours, seeping through from contacts in the police, pointed to the fact that Ray was not saying anything; that he just sat and stared at his interrogators.

As the newscaster uttered the first line, so all the speculation, along with any false hopes of a happy resolution, died.

"*Evrikame to ptoma tis Celias*" the announcer said and the subtitles came up in English at the bottom of the screen.

'We have found the body of Celia'.

Following immediately on this sentence the pictures flashed up of the police removing the body in a blanket, there below the cliffs at Aphrodite's Rock. Not people to be squeamish, the Cypriot T.V people showed the top half of the torso. They panned in on the mutilated face and showed the scarf tied tight around her neck. The people on the balcony recognized her by the unmistakable dark curls on the head and the colours of the neck scarf. As some broke out sobbing, Sampson, unable to release a tear yet, because the huge lump in his throat stifled him, stared at the setting of the burial place; the terrible irony of the lifeless body being carried up the beach to the imposing backdrop of the Goddess' rock.

He knew that now the evidence all seemed to point against Ray. All the gory details would come out in the Paphos courtroom soon enough. But there was something he sensed, that others might not, and that was that somehow the Goddess of Love, herself, was tied up in this. It was the dream of the villa in the hillside and a vista of sweeping hills down to the sea, where this Goddess was born, that lured the Dollys of this world in to Paphos.

She, the ancient protectress of the island, represented the dream. But there was a dark side to living in Cyprus and, Sampson now felt, a mysterious presence that lurked in the villages of the Troodos foothills where Aphrodite's temples had stood for more than three thousand years. It was a presence that many who lived in that area had sensed and one that he had increasingly become aware of, since he had come to live in Tremithousa.

The report in the Cyprus Mail, which appeared the next day and which Sampson read, as usual, in his accustomed corner of the taverna at Tremithousa, had pieced together the way the body had been discovered. The Cyprus fox had been the first to find Celia in her shallow grave just above the beach near *Petra Tou Romiou.* He had unearthed the hand and pulled the bony lifeless arm to one side to reveal the face. He had taken an exploratory bite at the most prominent item on the face, the nose. Then he had left, leaving his telltale paw marks in the sand. The shepherd who had come along three days later had found Celia's body and, realizing it was probably the woman everyone was looking for, had notified the authorities in Paphos.

A further report carried the story of Ray's confession. He had had cancer of the groin and his condition, or the medicines he had been taking, had left him impotent. Celia was no longer able to tell her side of the story but Ray had said that she taunted him on the fateful day about this and, after an ensuing tiff, there had been a struggle by the fireplace. She had slipped and fallen on the edge of the stone fire surround and a sharp edge had opened a large gash in the back of her head. He had tried to stem the blood by tying a scarf, acting as a tourniquet, around her neck. She had died in his arms.

As Sampson read this, regardless of the fact that he believed the whole story was not there, a wave of compassion swept over him not only for Celia but even for Ray and for the human condition in general.

The report continued: 'Detective Inspector Skourides took a statement from Mr Dolly to the effect that he panicked after his wife's death, thinking the whole scene looked incriminating against him. He had put her body in the Pajero late that night, and taken her out to the beach below Kouklia, a place that had been a favourite of theirs for picnics. There he had buried her.'

'He returned to Paphos and reported his wife missing, first to the headmaster of the International School who had just returned to school after the half term break, then two days later to the Paphos police.'

Sampson remembered the morning in question; the ashen white face of Ray that everyone simply associated with a sleepless night; the words of reassurance that people had offered Ray; the general feeling of helplessness as the day wore on and no news came in from Celia.

After reading the details of the arrest and the charges that had been placed against Ray, John Sampson put the newspaper down to reflect on the whole notion of fate. No wonder the ancients put so much store on it and that their Gods and Goddesses were invested with the power to play games with lesser mortals. Life seemed to defy straight logic. Last week two friends of his were a warm and loving couple. Today one was dead and the other had been formally charged in connection with her murder.

EPISODE 5

The caves of Drepanum

The first time she had uttered her name, *Undiga,* he guessed it was northern European, German or Scandinavian perhaps. She had arrived on her own one evening at Akis and Soulla's taverna and she had sat down immediately at his table. She had heard tell of the great food and ambiance available in Tremithousa and had come to test it out on behalf of her clients, a small group of Norwegian tourists due to come out to Cyprus in a few days time. She had asked questions about the day's catch of floral specimens he had laid out on the table. Then she had moved on to him. At first he had been a little reticent. Only a couple of months before he had felt the awakenings of deeply hidden desires when he had met Margo, the Channel 4 producer, in exactly the same spot. A week with her had only underlined how the chrysalis had not yet come out of its cocoon. He knew it would take time for him to forget the trauma of the divorce and to distance himself from the stiflingly academic world of Oxford.

If Margo had been attractive with a fascinating smile and the easy charm of the 'girl next door' then Undiga was simply a classic example of feminine beauty. The high cheek bones, deep Baltic-blue eyes and the tresses of fair hair that stopped just short of a perfectly rounded bottom, left him in no doubt that he was in the presence of a northern Goddess. As they had sipped their drinks, he his Keo beer and she her glass of Aphrodite white, he had found himself genuinely relaxing in her company. For seven months he had not been able to let himself relax like this. It was as though he had been hypnotized and was operating in an ethereal world in which her voice and look was the only one he could respond to. By the time she had got up to go, he had been thoroughly mesmerized.

Now, two days after the encounter, she had rung up the school where he worked two mornings a week helping with the biology. They hadn't actually planned to contact each other. He hadn't even given the number of the school. If it was to happen it would. But now when he'd taken the receiver he noted the rise in his pulse-rate when, in her North European cadence, tinged with a certain hint of matter-of-fact North American, she asked him how he was doing.

"Just thought I'd give you a buzz!"

Immediately the powerlink returned. The voice set off the hypnotic reaction. He felt as though he had known her always, a presence he had never tired of. She had talked in the taverna of her belief in fate and in reincarnation. His scientific background had forced him only to smile indulgently at that.

"Undiga, how about a drink this afternoon at 2 pm—at the harbour in Kato-Paphos. Stephanos' place where the pelican struts around outside? You can't miss it. Yes, opposite the yachts. You can make it for two thirty? Fine, I'll have a cold spritzer ready for you."

"That sounds pretty good to me. But I've got to be back in Limassol for six." The American tones in her voice came, he remembered her saying, from her five years spent at Harvard studying International Law. She hadn't been ready for a closed office yet . . . decided to have a year in the sun, running tours for a Norwegian travel company.

"OK don't stand me up will you?"

"And would I do that to you, John?"

He was just about to put the phone down when she came back on.

"Oh and John have you got any of those flower specimens at school with you?"

"Yes I've got some Sand Daffodil bud shoots with me today. I'm showing them to the kids!"

"Good. Bring me one will you! I would like to get it growing in my flat"

"I'll see what I can do for you"

She had gone off the line. He put down the receiver. The school secretary was looking over at him with a knowing smile on her lips. She must have been watching his reactions on the phone. Suddenly he felt very transparent.

The rest of the morning he was on a high, floating in and out of the lab, even proffering a smile at Loulakis whose sour expression usually made him feel like making a dash for the door. At two o'clock he went over to the biology darkroom. He wrapped the tiny faint brown and yellow daffodil in soaked cotton wool, dropped it into an envelope and marked it 'Undiga'.

The rendez-vous took place at exactly two thirty. One beer and one spritzer turned into two of each, as they watched the yachts tie up beside the Venetian castle that guarded the entrance to Paphos harbour. She thanked him for the flower and said she would take great care of it. The Sand Daffodil was pretty rare and this he had impressed upon her. He found himself fixing another date. They would hire a motorbike and strike off along the coastline on Saturday to Drepanum, where white chalky sea-caves provided a dramatic setting, backed as they were by the high woods of Akamas.

Until today Sampson had been on a low. It had been Mrs Dolly's death that had done it. The whole school had been mourning the loss of the junior headmistress but he himself had felt strongly let down—exactly by who, he wasn't sure. The matter-of-fact scientist within him should have simply accepted the facts as told by the 'Cyprus Weekly,' when it had all come out two weeks after the murder. Her husband, Ray's, cancer of the groin had made him temporarily impotent. She had taunted him in a moment of frustration. Then the struggle by the fireplace. The pretty head gashed by the mountain stone Ray had so carefully laid in the dream villa two years previously. Most of the British community were saying: "Wasn't it all just terrible!" and leaving it at that. Sampson, however, knew, with another more instinctive part of the brain, that it was the dream itself that was responsible, that dream personified by the Goddess he had begun to think of as a dangerous temptress.

Now here he was himself, being led like a sacrificial lamb to the altar of beauty. Undiga had reminded him directly of Botticelli's representation of Venus. Strange, he thought, how a Mediterranean painter had come up with such a fair Northern version of the Goddess. That fairest of hair, those long legs effusing femininity. The subtle mixture of the wake-up and get-sexy-look and the remoteness of the bookish librarian. Perhaps that was what Undiga would turn out to be: lawyer-librarian in the morning, sweet harlot when the sun went down. Imagination, he knew, was a powerful stimulant. He found himself, to his surprise, desiring this woman and wanting to know all of her.

By motorbike, the dusty coastal track to Drepanum was just passable. It deteriorated as it led on towards the protected beach at Lara where a Greenpeace ship had been attempting to divert attention away from the shy sea turtles. The *Careta Careta,* as they were called in Greek, had laid their eggs there for as long as anyone could remember.

The Harley Fatboy 900 allowed you to skirt the difficult sandy patches by riding rough upon a thin line of worn rocks until a firmer wider stretch came up. Sampson was enjoying the rough terrain. Her long legs were wrapped close to his, her hair lost to the wind behind. Now and again a few strands would come forward as the wind changed and she would tickle his neck and ear with them as she put her head forward on to his shoulder, to allow herself to go with the bumps in the track.

Cyprus was an island of reawakening. Stirrings deep within could testify to that. Yesterday darkness reigned: today this. The girl on the pillion seat was so natural. An easy sensuality lay upon her. She didn't need to try at all.

The white chalk caves of Drepanum opened up as they came around the headland, six kilometres from Corallia Bay. The afternoon sun came through the larger of the three great arches which lay in front of the corridor-like structures. It turned the sea encompassed by it into shimmering gold, as though announcing the beginning of an ancient and awesome ceremony.

She did not say the expected. No sighs of wonder. Instead she let her lips rest gently on the nuke of his neck and it felt very right and very good. The first intimate touch with her mouth. It made him turn his head, only to have another sweet kiss blown down his left ear.

'*Ta matia sou sto dromou!*" she shouted laughing. She'd been practicing her Greek too and he knew, if he didn't really keep his eyes on the road as she was telling him to do, they'd be over the top of the steep precipice from where the track dipped down to the sea-caves.

If there was anywhere on this island where the Goddess might have retreated so long ago, after having received her votive offerings for the day from the pilgrims at her altar at Ieroskipos on the other side of Paphos, it would have been here. You could walk into the sea a little way then disappear down a labyrinth of tunnels, water dancing high to your thighs, sun shafting through the slats in the vaulted ceilings and playing on the chalky walls. It might have been her palace and hand-maidens and royal play-mates would have lain provocatively as Undiga did now, naked, sated, watching as Sampson tried to unlodge a small octopus clinging to the wall two foot below the water surface.

When he emerged he splashed an invisible octopus on to her thighs. She screamed then laughed, as she began to frame the question she needed to ask him.

"Are you happy, John?"

He could not bring himself to answer, thinking of those dark nights, only a month or so back, when he would stop the car and lie out by the well known tourist spot, Aphrodite's Rock, on his way to or from a function in Larnaca or Nicosia. A Persian painting he had once seen had superimposed itself on his imagination during those quiet, even dangerous, nights.

"I think I am, how to say it, ... beginning to find a direction," he retorted.

The painter had been present at the exhibition and had pointed out to him, personally, how the theme was a classic Persian dream. The dreamer lay in beautiful surroundings looking out to a lit sky wherein a genie, blue and gold against the darker background, held an image of the recumbent figure and smiled back down at him. The painter had let him look through a magnifying glass at the detail. The way the paint had been applied, had partly created a 3D effect: and the artist had explained: "This is how we weave our magic in Persia, you see, and it has a lot to do with colour!".

"They were lonely, dangerous nights," he said out loud.

Undiga asked "Which ones?" and he was immediately brought back to her blue eyes, more magicking than anything in the painting or in the interpretation of the dreams he had attempted in his efforts to find his inner equilibrium.

Since he didn't answer, she continued:

"Those were the nights before I came along," and she cradled his head in a mothering gesture. "Now it's all going to change." The kiss that came was soft and subtly female. Her shapely breasts allowed her nubile form to contrast with the flat chalky bed upon which she lay.

Somewhere, distant, he could hear the tinkle of bells that announced a goat-herd. He wondered if it was the old shepherd he had encountered on his flower-hunting expedition two months back, now leading his flock, just as his father had done before him, to fresh pastures way up above them, on the cliff.

Undiga moved languorously into the water, allowing her body to fall into the four foot of water six paces away, the Botticelli tresses, that so defined her, lying behind her on the crystallized surface of the Mediterranean.

"Yes," he said to himself. "I'm happy at this moment. If only I could stretch it for an eternity."

From where he was in the shade of one of the sea-caves, he could not see, but definitely could hear, the foot on the arch above him. The scraping of the limestone now let the powder float down through the minute cracks in the ceiling of the cave. Undiga was out naked in the sea and here was a stranger above him. He was up in a flash, running down the corridor to the left where he knew the feet were moving forward. Once out into the light and now, at about six feet depth, just about treading water, he could see that Undiga, who had finished her swim, had climbed up onto a rock about twenty yards out into the bay and was sunning herself, long legs bent up in front of her.

Sampson swam out far enough to be able to look back to the top of the sea arches. Then he saw him motioning wildly to Undiga. A peasant farmer maybe, perhaps just another shepherd-huge brown working hand telling her to come back to the shore. She had not noticed. Then the man above was shouting something in his thick Cypriot tones.

"*Ta vouna, proseche! Kindinos!*"

Sampson knew only two of the words. One meant 'waves'; another 'danger'. He turned his head to look out toward the rock and saw the advancing curve of the towering waves.

Panayiotis Charalambous had been a forestry worker for twenty five years now, but never had he seen a naked woman, foreign at that, lying out so temptingly as this one now did. She appeared to be alone and he came out from the cover of the greenery to descend the path that led down towards the caves. Curiosity led him. He had heard about all the Northern European women who lay out topless at *Ayia Napa*, on the other side of the island. His nephews were always running off down there, reporting back in the taverna at *Drosia*, getting all the men worked up with their intimate descriptions. As he descended, however, he noticed the myriad white tops dancing beyond the rock where the female lay. Earlier, from the vantage point of the high outcrop above *Amathea*, he had noticed the sea-wind changing direction as it could do so suddenly in the Eastern Mediterranean. He had said to himself:

"The fishermen won't be putting out this afternoon. This is the *Boreas*. Nobody would go out in that."

Too many memories back in the village of fine young men lost on days when, inland, it was as calm as the smile on Aphrodite's statued face in the museum in Paphos. Panayiotis knew he had no time to lose. Bounding down the remaining fifty yards of pathway, he was on top of the larger of the sea caves where he knew he could run out a little way— perhaps shout to her—warn her.

Sampson had also begun to shout:

"Undiga—Undiga—get in here!"

The waves, that had appeared to come from nowhere, were now building high behind her rock and were preventing her from hearing. Then she changed position slightly, caught John's bobbing form and saw the look of intent on his face as the crashing sea unseated her and flung her forward in his direction. She saw the dark swirling depths moving in, dived like a dolphin so the top roller would not upend her and dash her against the rocks which dotted the bottom. Up she came for air just as the wash fell back. Feet touched bottom and she was racing for the cave, back into which John had just been buffeted. As she ran, the large brown hand of a Cypriot peasant now motioned from the edge of the promontory above. As she reached the mouth of the tunnel, she heard him yelling at her to get out: *"Grigora! Exo!"*

Inside, John took her by the hand and they raced back towards the flat bed of chalk where they had five minutes ago lain together. Undiga managed to quickly pull on the stringy bottom of her bikini. They needed an exit and spotting the now darkening light of day pointing on to a small patch of beach, they veered off at a right angle to the tunnel by which they had walked out to sea ten minutes before. No more than two strides had they taken than the huge black wave, that had been gathering its full strength behind Undiga's sunning rock, had now deluged the outcrop of stone and was thundering toward the entrance to the cave. Ten to twelve feet high and curling at the upward perimeter, it appeared like a mad woman, a huge Medusa, hair in disarray, lips gnarled, screaming through the corridor, as if in for the kill.

Sampson had time only to catch Undiga's trailing arm, as she tried to slide her way out of the cave, and hurtle her back against a cranny in the wall of the chalky passage. The monster roared past. Now, here in the confines of the hollowed-out sea cave, the great wave had reached its sanctuary, following upon the millions before which had sculpted the labyrinth of Drepanum. The spray rebounded, cutting into their skin as if a thousand tiny nails had been driven in. At last the mass of water rolled back but, no doubt, this was only to gather reinforcement for another assault.

From above, a voice could be heard, urging them up to a largish gap in the roof where a rock-chimney, shaped somewhat awry, led up.

"Exo, Exo, Par Etho."

Both John and Undiga's newly acquired Greek vocabulary stretched to the word '*exo*'; it simply meant get out! Sampson looked for a way that could offer finger and footholds. It was smooth sheer chalk—but there was no way out but this. Placing the small of his back against one wall of the chimney, he made Undiga understand that he would shuffle his way up by pushing hard with his feet against the opposite wall.

"You'll have to watch me go up and imitate exactly what I do," his voice echoed through the eerie silence that had followed on, after the crash of the sea had subsided. He started off, gripping as best he could on the chalk with his knuckles, his back arched hard against one wall, his feet walking the perpendicular rock face opposite.

Panayiotis had seen what was happening as the two had retreated from the sea. He had run, searching for a reasonable sized opening in the ceiling of the cave, found one, shouted out his warnings telling them to get out, though he doubted they, being *Englesi* or something similar, would understand. The hole was still not big enough for a human to crawl through, so Panayiotis applied his big black mountain boot to it and, because it was chalk, it began to widen and give way. He then urged them on again for he could see something moving down below:

"Grigora, paidia, grigora"

Sampson was making some progress, taking some strength from the fact that he could see the a vague outline of the Cypriot moving about above him. For the moment, all was silent. Perhaps the sea would give them enough respite to get up and out. The boot appeared through the opening above him sending down a shower of white powder. It fell in his eyes and made him splutter. Half-blinded as he was, he was just able to reach for and grasp the boot which still kicked on the chalk. His head followed the boot up through the freshly widened aperture. Then a large, strong hand was around one wrist and he was pulled free.

Looking back down, he could see that Undiga had begun her ascent. Not an easy climbing shuffle, this one. At least he'd had some experience of rock-climbing and chimney work back in his undergraduate days. She was only a third of the way up and she seemed exhausted. Fear alone would be numbing her. He tried to think quickly. No rope, how about a sheet? No sheet. It had to be a shirt! Since his was by now washed out with the tidal assault, he motioned to the Cypriot to take off his shirt, then took the scarf from around the woodman's neck. He knotted them speedily but very firmly together. The Cypriot took it from him and dropped the makeshift rope down to Undiga who gratefully caught hold of it.

"Wrap it tight around one wrist," Sampson yelled out to her as he took over at the mouth of the escape hatch. She didn't discuss it, was just in the process of banding it round her left wrist shouting back:

"I've got . . . it!"

The final syllables were lost to the enormous crack of the new wave that had gone in, this time for the finish. The men standing on top recoiled, as vapour and spume raced through every outlet in the roof. The sky had, within the last fifteen minutes, turned a dirty angry grey, the sea had become a raging beast. Only minutes ago Undiga had been out there lying in the . . .

Sampson could stand it no longer. Overtaken by a mixture of rage and bewilderment, the shock of the sudden mortal danger they found themselves in stripped him, for a moment, of his normal equilibrium. He ran to the edge of the cliff and, cupping his hands, yelled out through the spray and mist to sea:

"You bastard! You jealous bitch . . . !"

He hoped she could hear it, that 'Goddess' you could confuse with a devil-witch and who had haunted his dreams since his very first day in Cyprus.

But where was Undiga? The last blast must have blown her off the chimney wall, perhaps swept her away. As the spume settled, he peered quickly down the boxed-in aperture. She'd been knocked off the chimney all right—was left spinning like a circus acrobat—the shirt and scarf rope, incredibly, still holding her and even more incredibly the salted face of Panayiotis staring down the jaws that had just spat torrents of sea water at him. He was still holding on. Now moving one hand over the other, the Cypriot pulled up Undiga, wild-eyed and frightened at the end of her lifeline. Her breasts were still bare, so she attempted to cover them with one arm, as she awkwardly scrambled over the rim of the opening. She hauled herself to her feet and fell into Sampson's grateful embrace.

"What the hell happened?" she whispered, through her breathless tight lips.

It was only when they had profusely thanked Panayiotis—this simple peasant man had no doubt saved their lives—that Sampson could bring himself to answer Undiga's question. As they watched the forestry worker retreat up the sharp slope that led to the Akamas high road above, the botanist found his reply.

"She came for us, Undiga! She came to get us. She's a jealous bitch!"

"What do you mean, John.? Do you really think there is someone out there brooding, waiting for a chance to get us?"

"The logical thinking side of me doesn't want to believe it, Undiga, but I've never, in all of my life, felt such a presage of danger as I have done since the day of my arrival in Paphos; never felt the presence and power of the ancient divinities as I have here in the Akamas. I fear that Aphrodite will jealously attack those, like ourselves, who inadvertently venture on to what she might regard as her stamping ground."

As they dried out and put on the fresh shorts and T shirts that they had left in the saddlebag of the 900, Undiga calmed him.

"John, how could you allow a mythological figure to overtake your imagination like this. If anything, we should be grateful. Providence sent us the Cypriot. We would never have got out without him. Nature has its quirks and times when it doesn't follow the usual laws. It was that kind of day today. But we were lucky and I got a feeling we will be lucky always."

With that she kissed him briefly but directly on the lips and then mounted onto the rear seat of the motorbike.

"*Pame.* Lets go!"

Sampson, only temporarily appeased, kicked the starter into life and pulled away in the direction of Paphos.

EPISODE 6

The well of Tsada

"It should be about here."

He pointed to the rough map of the area in his hand, tracing out a circle which bordered with Rosie's garden walls and that of her southern neighbour. They were looking for the main artesian water spring at Tsada, a village in the Paphos mountains, which guarded the highest point of the area known as the *Eparchia Paphitiki* or Paphos District Council. As John's eye followed the direction south, he could see the cafeneion and the church perched just to the right of the road that had been dynamited through in the 1970s. Now at the start of the new millenium he could make out a twist in the freshly widened road which led in a swoop through mountain vineyards down to Polis and Latchi.

As they made their way round the walls and back to the gate of her house, Rosie ran through her story. She had been looking to make her nest there for years but had never been able to find just the right spot. Eventually, a '*mantri*' or goat house had come up for sale. Everyone went for the goat houses in those days. A century before they had been inhabited by people. Then, since many had fallen into disrepair, they were used to house goats and donkeys. They were cool two foot-thick stone wall structures that guarded against the sickening heat of summer and the sometimes quite sharp winds lashing down from the northern peaks of Troodos in winter. So they had reverted to human habitation. The stone shell would be completely cleared out, only the walls remaining, and then rooms would be added on

Before Rosie had come to take over her *mantri*, Kyria Evangelia had been one of the last to leave her traditional abode and had continued to live there well after the rest of her generation had left for the suburbs of Paphos.

"I don't blame her. Look at she was enjoying! One hell of a dramatic view over that large dappled pond they call the Med, below us here!".

The old lady had wanted to turn it over to the animals, just about the time when the *mantris* became popular second home targets for ex-patriot people retiring from Europe or from the Gulf. Evangelia had been forced to give it up by old age; had gone to live with her sister, but for years she never would sell her property, despite pressure from, mainly English, expats, tempting her with hard cash. Somehow, however, she had taken a liking to Rosie and had led her through the overgrown garden. They made an unlikely couple, Rosie a lanky Londoner, she herself a wizened four feet eight inches. The garden had been large but overgrown with tough elephant grass. The few plants the goats had not eaten provided splashes of colour, but it was the views through the stout abbey portal, that sat incongruously at one end of the garden, that had taken Rosie's fancy so much and Evangelia knew she would have to give it to her.

There had been an Abbey here, Evangelia had explained, dating from the time of the Lusignan occupation of Cyprus but the earthquake of 1949 had taken it down, all except one arch still engraved with the royal Lusignan lion rampant. The suggestion now was that the garden behind the portal was a hallowed place.

Now, Sampson and Undiga were sitting admiring this very archway, one of those evenings scented with the thyme the villagers were throwing on their Saturday night fires.

"*Ella*", he heard Rosie say and her maid, a local village girl, led them up the stone pathway that took them to a now disused well. This was the centre-piece of the garden.

When the two guests had taken their seats on the stone covered surround to the well, Rosie continued her story of how she had bought the house and of how Evangelia had been the local "magissa" or "wise-woman". She had baked the bread in the same oven as she did the Cypriot delicacy, *kleftiko*. Many had come to buy her bread, sometimes to take it away to use at Sunday mass when the Pappas would stamp it with the holy sign of the lamb. She had also managed to contain certain "devils" down the well with her incantations. Rosie continued her story.

"You know, at Easter, how the orthodox priests recite in the churches the biblical phrase: 'Get behind me Satan.' The faithful, of course, now fully believe the devil has been banished from their lives. Evangelica would, however, put on her own service, even though she would have attended the Orthodox church as well. All Cypriot women had to attend under pain of being ostracised. She would come home from the eleven o'clock mass, give people bread and herbs and incant over the well: "Go down Satan, down to the depths of this well!" The villagers now really believed he, the devil, was well out of harm's way, relegated as he was to the bottom of the well."

"Then she would distribute her potions and unguents made from *sinaposporoi*—black seeds from the green *sinapi* plant used for healing wounds and snake bites. They also came to take the hot cups for draining out a fever or *tsai tou elmou*, a herbal tea imported all the way from the Peloponesus in Greece, to settle stomach ache and keep people regular. She had a knowledge of herbs and of what could be extracted from the locally grown plants and flowers and because of this the *magissa* had some cure to offer for each and every ailment."

Sampson was a highly respected botanist in Britain. He had the grandiose title of Professor Emeritus of Botany at Oxford. However, as he sat down at the small table beside the well with his glass of *raki* in his hand, he did not know what was more intoxicating, the heady whiff of mountain magenta that conjured up one of Evangelia's healing sessions and which the cool night brought to his senses, or the extra strength *raki* which, as each mouthful went down, made him smack his lips together in an attempt to cool its bite.

One further element cloaked the night with pure magic—the presence of Undiga. His newfound love, so foreign to this place, made a natural contrast with the village girl who had come out with the rakis and had just now seated herself on the rim of the well. Beauty was in both of them—sparkled blue and olive brown through two pairs of eyes. The third female in the garden, Rosie, bespoke an easy grace, redolent of the best of British expatriate women. She was an attentive and charming hostess and could make everyone feel included, even the village girl who helped her out around the house and outbuildings. There, on the outer perimeter of the garden, the Cypriot girl tended a few hens and two pigs which were being fattened for Easter.

"Oh, what's that?" cried Undiga, pointing to the trestled vines which ran like a roof a metre above their heads. Sampson looked up.

"See? Fluffy white bellies of what looks like two baby squirrels".

"What, on earth, are they?" Sampson enquired of Rosie.

Rosie had become so used to these animals scampering through the vines that, at first, she did not recognize what was causing the stir. She turned from putting down the *meze* of salad and pork delicacies, the taramasalata and the hummous, on the stone table. Her guests were peering up through the light of the single blue candle she had provided.

"Oh, they're my little pets, my tree mice."

"Tree mice!" cried Undiga in delight "I didn't know they existed".

"Their habitat is mostly in Indonesia but this pair is unusual. They came here from the rain forest of Borneo. Bob, my husband, brought them back from one of his trips there. Well, you met him last time, didn't you? He's an engineer, expert on dams; travels all over. Yes, these little girls have survived well here. They sleep in the washing machine at night". How quaint, thought Sampson, but where else in Cyprus more appropriate to spot unusual animals than in this garden, where Evangelia's spells seemed to linger still?

A flash of lightning swept through the starless night and a deep rumble followed almost immediately. The young Cypriot girl crossed herself quickly and ran quickly for the house. Sampson moved over to the well, alone, as Rosie took Undiga by the arm to show her the house and rooms. It had been gearing up to rain in those mountains for some days now. When it arrived, the sleeting water would wash down over the whole Troodos range. The storm would come as quickly as the wave had attacked them at Drepanum.

He walked over to the mouth of the well and looked down it. The well's interior was dark, providing an impression of great depth. Sampson reflected on how we all kept our devils subdued. Plato had written of his theories of opposites; you needed a devil to feel the presence of God. You need to see the dark side of a Goddess nature in order to respect her great beauty. As he stared down the walled recess, he was overtaken by a great desire to meet her 'in person,' or so to speak, to stare into her eyes; to see what she actually wanted of him.

The first huge pellets fell, chunks of ice which bounced off his head, clunked down the well and made him dash inside for cover where he found the Cypriot girl laughing uproariously, as she taught Rosie and Undiga some of the earthier Cypriot words.

"My God" he shouted to Rosie over the noise of the storm. "Those chunks of ice are lethal. Have you seen anything like this before?"

Even as he spoke the plinth lay littered with ice.

"Oh, it happens," Rosie replied. "We are so high up here, we get all types of weather. One year the hailstones were twice as thick as that. Two years ago, to be precise, huge icy hail spoiled the crops completely. No Paphos wines produced that year and it killed two people; knocked down two old peasant ladies who were out working on the vine teraces, then froze them as they lay there. The following day, a whirlwind span round the Paphos bay, all connected with this strange cold spell. It swept through the orange groves along by the coast and whisked away the glass houses used for growing vegetables."

"Rosie, am I right or am I wrong? Is this not the strangest place on earth? Sudden polar-like storms, followed by beautiful weather, calm seas suddenly turned into tidal waves which dash into ancient caves? You know, we nearly got ourselves killed the other week at Drepanum! A lover suddenly killed his loved one. There is something weird in this Paphos area, isn't there.?"

The urgency in his question demanded a sympathetic response. Rosie turned, half smile on her face:

"What can you expect in Aphrodite's country, John? She's a woman. If she were alive today she would probably be a power-dresser. She'd take great glee in making big men cry."

John stared back.

"I know you might think I'm stupid, Rosie, or gone a little *trianta grammaria*, a Tremithousa nutcase, that's what they call him isn't it? You know! Only got thirty grams of brain when you should have fifty!"

"John, that well at the end of the garden represents it all. I'll explain. You're not the first person to feel the presence of the myth here. The local fishermen have a prayer to her—to Aphrodite—before they go out. Believe me there are some swirling eddies out there that would swallow you whole. The well has it too, paganism and fear . . . somehow a grudging respect for the ancient myth. There is the primitive in all of us. You've been able to get away from the top table of Brasenose and the Latin grace and you've opened yourself to real feelings. You've come to a land where, there can be no doubt, charm blends in with the fearsome, the modern with the ancient."

Sampson stepped back and sat on one of the traditional Cypriot straw stools beside Undiga. Rosie had put it all in a nutshell, so sensibly, so sufficiently. He'd been too involved, at too close quarters, to even notice how changes had occurred in the course of the last six months. His sense of smell had heightened, life had become more intense. He'd breathed atmospheres laden with a heady blend of history and mythology. Look at him! He'd even started talking to Aphrodite, looking out for her, half expecting her to respond. That day, he'd gone looking for the rare orchids up in Akamas, he'd allowed the instinctive in him to take over.

Undiga put her head on his shoulder and looked up at him with a smile.

"You see John, relax! We both of us have been getting too wound up, starting to believe it was really her who was after us. What happened in those caves, my sweet, has been happening for millions of years. The sea gets up a swell and bashes that little piece of coastline particularly well. Hence the sea caves. They have been hollowed out in that fashion and are in themselves beautiful. We just happened to be there to witness one linked event in a very long natural cycle."

The hailstone had stopped as abruptly as it had started. Rosie got up, took him by the arm and led him out.

"Come on, Undiga. Follow us. You too, Maria, *kai fere to kouvadaki!*"

The girl picked up the bucket, as she had been instructed, and followed them out.

Over to the well went the procession, feet crackling on the enormous lumps of ice that had fallen from a dark sky above. Sampson imagined that this was the kind of deluge people would pray deliverance from in the Anglican services of his youth—on St. Swithins day, if he remembered correctly! The line in the litany went something like . . . 'and deliver us from all deluge and deliver us from great flood.'

Acting on instructions from Rosie, Maria clipped the pail on to a hook which was at the end of the chain wrapped above the well. Soon it was noisily banging against the deep walls as it sank ever deeper. The echo of the bucket became a measure of the depth, as it seemed to continuously come from further away.

"What are you doing, Rosie, trying to knock the devil out?" Undiga asked with dry mirth.

"Something like that," replied Rosie. "Trying to knock unknown ghosts out of John here."

Then the hollow splash, as bucket hit water deep in the bowel of this strange mountain and now the long pull up. Maria motioned to John to help. The weight of the chain was adding to the laborious job of hauling the water up. Sampson was aware that he was repeating inwardly *kato satane* as Evangelia had no doubt done so many times in days gone by.

Thirty seconds later it was Rosie who spoke, as the rim of the bucket tippled water over their feet.

"This is it, my dears. This is the water that cured the villagers. It's clean, it's pure and therapeutic. The devil that Kyria Evangelika kept so very much alive stopped people tampering with it, you see. Quite a useful devil, he was!"

She took up four raki glasses from the table where the meze still awaited them and filled them with the cold water from deep in the earth:

"Here's to a healthy respect for nature, no matter how it's represented!"

They clinked glasses and drank. Sampson felt the cleansing flush, as the raki he'd earlier been drinking had now left the taste buds and was replaced by a deep and refreshing coolness.

He wondered whether this would be a turning point. Beauty and the good things were all around; he could appreciate them now. He suddenly had a great desire to laugh out loud, long and lustily. As he began to break the night air with his chuckles, Rosie and Undiga joined in and smiled, as doctors would when they might witness an unexpected cure for a chronic malaise.

EPISODE 7

North to Kyrenia

From where he stood, on the central spot of the ancient stone stage, his voice spun round the arena and came back to him, the metallic ring of man-fashioned words sharply reflected by earth's oldest matter.

"I think this coming summer the King of Sicilia means to pay Bohemia the visitation which he justly owes him."

He had been practising the lines for a few weeks now since he had volunteered to take on the part of the Lord Camillo in Shakespeare's 'The Winter's Tale' to be put on at Kourion outdoor Greek theatre in July. The title seemed strangely inappropriate, this warm March day at Salamis in Northern Cyprus. The theatre, now unused yet in such excellent condition, had a sad feel, as though the ghosts of Euripides and Sophocles dwelt there, pining out their tragedies, a slight wind carrying their *oimais* around deserted seating.

Sampson was nursing his words of self-pity today, his *oimai*, his call of grief. Undiga was going back to Norway and, although she had warned him she would need to go back to tend to her sick mother, it was still a shock that now only a day remained.

He shifted very slightly to the left and continued, trying to forget.

"They were trained together in their childhood and there was rooted between them such a friendship which cannot choose to branch now".

From high up at the back of the terraced seating, Undiga waved her arms and gave the thumbs up. She attempted to shout something back down but it didn't carry.

"Ah," thought Sampson. "It is true that it only happens on that small spot. The perfect inner circle. That is where the resonance is pure and the feed-back is at its optimum." He had read that, at Epidaurus ancient theatre, in the Peloponesus peninsula in Greece, a person standing at the back of the auditorium could hear a pin drop on that central spot.

He needed her close, so close they could both hear each other's whispers. He moved quickly forward from the spot and ran up the stepped stone to where she waited. Taking her in his arms he looked over her left shoulder and through to the spreading ruins of the once great city of Salamis and to the sea which lapped at its eastern. boundary. There was nobody there. Just themselves and this majesty. The Turkish Cypriot communities did not readily seek out the ancient. Survival in the present age took up all their time. The Greek community had not been able, till gaining very restricted access very recently, to cross the United Nations controlled border

Being "outsiders," Undiga and he had been able to get through both Greek and Turkish formalities, with a warning by the Greek authorities to return by six that evening. Then they'd driven the old cream Volvo Amazon, that Sampson had picked up in Kato Paphos, some months before, for seven hundred euros, through the miles of yellow flowers predominant now in May, the Pendactylo Mountain Range providing a steep backdrop to what could have otherwise been a Monet painting. Here and there, flashes of red and purple anemones, contrasted with the yellow daisies. When Undiga had marvelled at the vividness of colour, John was able to tell her that these anemones had been believed in legend to be the blood of Adonis, when he was killed by a wild boar at the behest of Aphrodite.

"Now here we are at one of the most ancient monuments to Greek culture", thought Sampson. "Its empty of visitors and it is truly a captivating place."

Unfortunately, however, the idea that this beautiful girl was going away in two days time invaded him with a sense of grief and loss. He had only just begun to feel fully alive again. She had played more that her fair share in that process. But, now, she had to go. Her mother was sick, she'd told him earlier in the car, but there was another reason she needed to tell him.

"I've got to go, anyway, John. I've got to get started on my career. I can't just keep on floating and drifting. I want to be something for your sake too."

He answered her gently, so his words passed like warm breath by her right cheek:

"About that drifting business, Undiga. You can, you know,! You can just keep on floating and drifting. Don't be like me. I was determined to make a professional name for myself by becoming knowledgeable about photographs of rare flora. I became literally a bookworm regaling my fellow dons at the high table of Brasenose College with names that sounded impressive because they were lengthy and in Latin. I kept my career and my students always bought my most recent books. I existed in a sort of cocoon. But, you know, I wasn't really living."

"What about your wife?" She had asked him this question before and he had always avoided answering. "Whatever happened to her?"

"Susan was too busy worming her way through history books; also not living. I crashed. Probably would have turned to some lethal dose of drugs and booze and gone to the wall. But the Fates led me on and I was washed up on the shores of this island, like Homer's Odysseus, a shipwreck in life, emotionally in tatters . . . ."

He stopped here because the memory was painful and he realised that perhaps he was lecturing, not on botany at least, but still lecturing. He just held her in close, her lips finding his and then she pulled gently back to speak again.

"Are you really still worried John? Worried that I won't come back; that you'll be left floundering alone on the shores of Cyprus? We've found something most people never do in a lifetime. This is for real. I don't intend to lose you John. I'm coming to get you soon".

Sampson reflected. Why indeed worry? What they had was strong, yet the primitive in him wanted to hold on . . . not to let go; the same primitive in him that had allowed him to discover his liberated self. Flowers and small shrubs had jumped out from the pages of books and taken shape and smell. Now he had seen all but the ten rarest. He had smelt them, nose down close to the earth. He had felt the presence of the protecting Goddess in those areas where the rare beauties grew.

Undiga had been, of course, the main sensory experience, all pervasive. Now, he did not want to let her out his sight. He needed to reach out and touch her often; never to lose her scent.

"Come on" she said. "Let's go for a walk along the beach here. We'll go along to the old port,shall we?"

Taking her hand, he led her down the grassy slope behind the theatre and soon they were wandering through Apollo's temple and what must have once been an altar or an eating table, the base of which remained clearly marked out on the ground, with six stone stools set around it. Then, suddenly, they were at the edge of the lapping waters of the Mediterranean. The water, the temples, the market place had been so close, even given that the sea may have moved in some fifty yards or so over two millenia.

"This port," John said, "may have been the one where Venetian ships would have moored at the time of their supremacy. Othello, according to Shakespeare, put in just up the coast at Famagusta to stem the threat from the Turkish Ottoman. They have a tower named after Othello there. The Venetians too would have marvelled at ancient glories just as now people marvel at the wonders created by Venice."

"I wonder if anyone will marvel at our office blocks and glass-fronted shops, fast-food shops and cinematic idols", Undiga added. "I doubt it somehow. They're transitory, not from Earth, no magic in them, not in harmony with the pulse of nature. You need that, John, the contact with things that grow out of earth and are fashioned with care from the earth and you need contact with the sea and the open sky and a healthy respect for the Gods & Goddesses, or let's call them powers, that protect nature."

He knew she was right. Although he respected the monotheistic religions, he could not help thinking that, once the old gods had been replaced by one supreme being, the rivers lost their protectors, the woods their Artemis, the sky its *Ouranos*. People no longer feared the vengeance of these divine patrons and began to abuse every manifestation of nature. The new God was somehow too remote and spiritual to do anything to promote the respect of nature.

She had stopped and taken off her sandals, the light cotton dress clinging to her lithe long legs. Then the dress fell in a neat pile at her feet

"I am going to miss that girl" he whispered to himself as she walked ahead out into the sea. She turned to look directly into his eyes, as if she had read his mind.

"You wait for me here in Cyprus John, because I love you. But right now ? Come on get in here!"

Moments later, he held her as the waves massaged them, every now and then sweeping their feet off the bottom and providing a rocking motion which gave Sampson the impression they were on some sort of aqueous swing. There was nothing imaginary, however, in the contorting limbs of the two lovers as they pulled one into the other. One armless statue of a Goddess guarded Salamis and them that day. Although the chipped bust looked out to sea in their direction, no one saw them, not even the Goddess, for she had the stare of the blind. His nose and mouth sank into her neck, before working down, sensuously, to her breast. The suction of the water and the buoyancy created new and highly erotic sensations.

An hour later, after drying off in the sun so that you could smell the salt on both of them, see it in patches on their arms and legs, they made their way to the Volvo Amazon which was parked on the track leading from the ruins down to the small beach where they had laid out their towels.

"Where to now Iannis?" She'd asked. She wanted to play with his name, and play with him, overtake him and be overtaken by him.

"Let's go to Kyrenia now", he said, "I've got an appointment near there".

As they pulled off down the road, she recalled, in her mind's eye, the first time she'd seen him, in the corner of the forecourt of that taverna in Tremithousa, with his Panama pulled down to shade his eyes. She remembered how he had struck an interesting figure. Then, when they'd talked across the three tables that took up the tiny forecourt, she'd noticed his eyes, deep and clever and she had nearly thought strong, until the glimpse of sadness and hurt had suddenly come through. She remembered being interested enough to hear he was looking for wild flowers; she liked men who worked with nature. But then she'd discovered, over the weeks she'd got to know him, that although he was earthy, he was also sort of locked up still, in the stuffy corridors of college life. Too late! She'd been smitten through. She had known it on that first night. A flush of colour had invaded her fair skin. She had gone a deep red and a tingling sensation had travelled straight down to the pit of her stomach. When he'd reacted the way he did at Drepanum, possessed her and then shown that he too needed her, she'd realised that she had found what she was looking for.

She'd go home to the fiords, start her career, look after her mother and either he'd come and live with her soon or she'd come see him every two months or so if he stayed in Cyprus.

"Make sure we turn right out of Famagusta for Kyrenia, Undiga. It should be marked the N1 but Kyrenia will be in Turkish—so look out for *Kyrniz*".

She now had the map spread out on her lap and allowed the aged soft leather of her seat to mould her back into comfort.

"What's up there then?" she ventured.

"Well there's a harbour—a very beautiful one and I've got a lady to see there!".

"Ah, an old flame, perhaps" she added quickly.

"Just an acquaintance with a secret" he grinned back.

Kyrenia came into view at the steep—almost precipiced-ridge that formed the top of the Pendactylo range of mountains which shielded the little coastal town that had, before the Turkish invasion, been the centre of English expatriate life in Cyprus. Bellapaix, which had made famous in Laurence Durrel's *Bitter Lemons* lay nearby, its ruined Abbey some miles over to the right, as John and Undiga began the descent.

Twenty minutes later she took in her breath, as what must have been one of the most beautiful views in the Mediterranean unfolded before her. The harbour reminded her of a bowl, situated in an arc of jagged mountains that only accentuated the still blue above it because, as Undiga looked up from the table beside the yachts where they sat awaiting their salads and wine, she felt encircled by the majesty of the mountains with the placid sea behind her. A hot humidity pressed over the natural bowl but a slight wind eased it.

"We'll take this in for an hour or so" said Sampson, then we can call over to Bellapaix, where I'm told Mrs. Beeson, my old flame, will be able to show me something of great interest to me, botanically of course!.

Undiga, enjoyed his joking manner and remarked to herself how much his confidence and his humour had returned to him. She knew she had been the catalyst for this. It made her feel very good that this man, the one she knew she loved, was emerging, like the wings of a butterfly do from the pupa, before her very eyes. She smiled at him and this said it all.

A red waist-coated waiter descended the ten steps, Undiga counted them, down from the cafeteria which, like the others on the perimeter of the harbour, were raised above the customer seating area.

Different, these Turks! she thought. Very different from the Greek Cypriots. Darker, perhaps a better bearing to them, but slightly more ferocious eyes on them.

John Sampson was able to offer a *Tesliarkur*, as the waiter laid down the salad loaded with small green Cypriot olives and which had been well marinated in vinegar oil and the ever-present oregano. With it came several slabs of the white goat-cheese, the *fettah,* and plenty of crisp green lettuce and cabbage that had been cooled in their fridges. The wine had come from Turkey, a light fruity offering that slipped down so easily and gave Undiga the feeling she could just stay, right there in Kyrenia harbour, for ever and a day.

A couple of brandies were brought "gratis" and, once downed, the two ambled off up to where they had parked the car, half way up the hill.

Driving a large, lumbersome car, with no power-steering, that also dated a few decades back into the previous century, could be tricky enough in the best of conditions. But for John, following the Turkish signposts, as he manoeuvred the old Volvo through the narrow lanes with half a bottle of wine and a large brandy inside him and with a warm spring sunshine penetrating through the windscreen, proved more than a little tricky. On his knee he had the map that Miss Beeson's sister, a member of Larnaca Amateur Botanical Society, had given him after one of his lectures.

"I think Emily has something that fits the description in slide number twelve growing in her garden." She had come up to him excitedly after a lecture and slide show on rare flora he'd given at the Town Hall in Larnaca, about two weeks before.

"And she said she'd looked it up and it was supposed to be very rare!".

The picture one might have taken with a camera that day, from the door of Emily Beeson's cottage where she awaited them, was one that could have graced a photographic exhibition. The sea beyond the hill provided distant backdrop and more to the bright reds and whites of the bougainvillea in the garden forefront. Through the centre of the picture a beautiful big cream vehicle carrying a bearded man with a hat on. Beside him, the fair appearance of his partner contrasted with his, somewhat swarthy, appearance.

The car pulled to a stop beside Emily, a woman perhaps in her seventies, yet marked by a youthful conditioning, for she was bright eyed and smiling. Undiga looked behind her through the mass of spring flowers and the thought passed her mind: who could fail to look healthy, if they were to live in this most beautiful spot in Cyprus?

"You must be Professor Sampson then . . . ?"

"Yes. Emily isn't it? Pleased to meet you, and this is Undiga".

"Please come in—I've made some tea for you".

It was like going up to a Cotswold Village for strawberries and cream on a blue sky, English summer, day. Sampson was reminded of his student days when he'd take time out from his studies at weekends to visit Burnt Norton and those other idyllic spots which lay north of Oxford. The strawberries today were imported but the whipped Turkish goat yogurt made a healthy substitute for the cream.

"John you go look around in the garden. See if you can find anything unusual down there under the fig tree. I'll show Undiga some of the photos we took when Lawrence Durrel and his brother, used to get together with my late husband and myself over at the Tree of Life, you know the little restaurant by Buffavento Castle that Lawrence so often makes reference to in 'Bitter Lemons'. The stuff of history now of course."

The women walked in to the parlour where touches of the home counties marked it out as the house of an English expatriate lady. Undiga noticed the way the net curtains hung just as they had done in the house in Sussex where she had been on an exchange from Bergen when she was a schoolgirl. They afforded a peep into the garden where the lawn had been immaculately manicured, probably, she thought, that very morning, ready for their visit.

From the kitchen, through the slats of glass framed in Cyprus pine, she followed John striding purposefully down the garden path that led to the spot where the fig tree brought shade to the bottom corner of the garden. She saw him reach up, pick a fruit from the tree, break its soft skin and suck out the cool fruit from within.

She turned to Mrs Beeson who was busy making the tea and asked,

"I imagine they must have been wonderful days then. Like a bygone age. Were they really like that?"

"Well if you read Durrel's book you get the feel of how slow the pace was. He seems to have extracted a magic from the Cyprus of the early nineteen fifties. I was just a young girl at the time, of course. It was quite a feat to get his house built; everything went so slowly. That's it over there on the hill."

At this she pointed through the bow window of the living room where, framed on the hillside, lay a white washed and red roofed villa.

"But, never forget, romantic viewpoints of life are often flawed. The darker side was reflected in the way women were treated here. They hardly ever got out of the fields. Then there were the EOKA troubles of the fifties which produced some horrific killings and a lot of torturing. Yes, apart from the sporadic violence, times were quieter. There was more room, less rush. People were satisfied with less. All times have their contrasts"

"John and I were at Salamis today. Not a soul around!"

'There's an example for you then. You have one of the best of ancient sites in the Greek world to yourselves on a beautiful Spring day. Yet the Greeks cannot visit their own heritage and nightly in Nicosia the Greek and Turkish soldiers call each other names to provoke an incident. Cyprus is a land of social and political contrasts"

The back door had opened and John had entered, carrying in his hand a small white flower with the roots still cloying to traces of the damp soil they had grown in.

"Ah so you found it, Professor Sampson. That's the one I saw in your book on Mediterannean Flora and my sister recognised it on one of your slides in Larnaca that day."

'Yes here it is. Cyclamen Cypraicum. Grows only in Cyprus. Not exactly the rarest of the flora found here but I am very happy to have a specimen, as it is still hard to find. Don't worry that I have hauled it out of the ground, Mrs Beeson. I'll pop it into a specially humidified bag that I keep in the back of the car, so that I can take it back to Paphos. Then it'll be transferred to a pot, containing rich soil taken from the Akamas, and special lights will be trained on it. I should be able to give you lots of new shoots, in about six weeks time, and I'll also give you shoots from the other rare babies I'm cultivating!"

Mrs Beeson looked pleased, as she imagined the very special rockery she could begin to have made under the fig tree.

An hour later, after taking tea and cucumber sandwichwes on the patio looking out toward Buffavento Abbey, the two visitors said their goodbyes. They had one hour to make it back to the Ledra Palace crossing in Nicosia. The daily curfew began at six every evening and, if visitors who had signed through that morning had not returned by that time, UN troops were notified and those visitors could find themselves at the centre of an international incident.

So, at precisely five forty five, the Amazon swept through, first past the Turkish soldiers then, after traversing the hundred yards or so of no man's land, the Greek Cypriot police and the United Nations observer post. Undiga was heading for Larnaca airport for ten thirty that night and John Sampson, after leaving her off there, would head westward, alone with his thoughts, to Paphos and his temporary home in the village of Tremithousa.

EPISODE 8

The *Odysseas*

A Scot's voice came out of the darkness.

"Are ye reedy there Jan?"

"Yes, a dooble tank filled today with 200 Eer Bar" . . . the stretched Dutch vowels sounded incongruous in the stillness of the Cypriot night . . . "that should give me wan 'oor at least at this depth."

Jan was clipping on his weight belt ensuring it was tight enough but not too constrictive to impede the back flip he would execute any minute now from the fishing vessel.

"Hand me the dive torch, Jock."

Jock threw him the heavily padded rubber torch that would light up the diver's way. At thirty meters depth, and at night, it would be darker than most people knew darkness could be. The celestial light would not penetrate even one metre below the surface. At thirty metres dark silence would conjure up a world of Orpheus.

The dive-knife, long and serrated, was the last thing to strap on. There, on his calf-muscle, he could feel the thin, cold security it provided.

"I'll just tag on that wee light to the front of the vessel, Jan—that way we'll no be taken for divers".

Jan surveyed the dark promontary of land before him.

"Looks preedy quiet oop there on the cleef!"

His voice seemed magnified out of all proportion in the circumstances, as though it were carried round the semi-circular bay faster than it had left the boat. The effect was one of temporary deafness that made him unblock his right ear with his finger. "Not a light of a car, only those bludy crickets that never shut oop!"

"Quiet or no I feel safer with that red lamp up on the bow—they'll think we're neet fishing!" the Scot retorted.

66

The latter got up and, stumbling over the heavy anchor and the coiled rope that lay on the port side, made his way to the bowsprit of the Cypriot fishing vessel, lit a match and applied it to the wick of the small red lantern. At night, all over the Mediterranean but especially in the Greek isles, you could see the reflection of these little red lamps, bobbing on the water to attract the fish. Looking as it did like any other Kri-Kri fishing vessel, the boat would not seem unusual, as it lay off the Pomos Point promontory, 60m N. East of Akamas. It would not attract too much attention.

The last thing the two men wanted was attention. They were good at avoiding it: had spent twenty years together since they'd met up in Britain on the North Sea Oil Rigs where they had become professional divers. They'd done five weeks on underwater welding and another ten on acetylene cutting processes. They'd made good money together but nothing like what had come rolling in over the last fifteen years or so, since they'd gone diving for other purposes.

Jock, although he had been drinking Scotch since lunch time, managed to load the spear-gun and put the safety catch on its spring. "Here ye are, Jan. Hope ye don't have to bloody use it but there are sharks in these waters! Now ye're ready. There's yer net and yer rope end for pulling the goodies up wi'. Good luck!"

Jan attached one end of an Octopus breathing hose to his mouth: the other was already on the regulator and a third hung free. He took three quick breaths to make sure all was working; then a quick thumbs up and he fell back into the bay of Pomos. Jock peered over the side to watch the torch point down to the depths. This time easy riches were within their grasp. He knew what was down there from the twenty minute 'rekky' dive on Wednesday afternoon when he and Jan had both gone down in a daylight search for the ancient treasure. He'd paid a lot for the information from his source in the Department of Antiquities and for the new sounding equipment he'd had to buy but it was going to be worth it. The first time he'd seen it he knew it was priceless! What was priceless to some meant quick riches to others. There was a growing market, Jock knew, in the United States, London, Paris and Amsterdam for Greek and Byzantine treasures. He'd helped fence some old icons across to New York after the Turkish Invasion when the Orthodox churches of Northern Cyprus had been looted and stripped.

The torchlight had gone from sight. His colleague really should not have gone down alone. Every pro diver knew this. But one of them had to stay up top to alert the other if other sea craft approached. In any case Jock was not really 'on form' today having drunk far too much of his favourite tipple. He took a seat on the small bench in the aft quarter and poured himself yet another real scotch—Single Malt, 15 years old—a luxury he would not do without. As he took the first wee dram, he thought;

"Ah well. Ma ould Dutch friend will manage it. Weight's no problem in the deep blue sea!"

John Sampson had had some difficulty getting the pegs of his tent into the strong clay ground, parched as it was now that the Cyprus summer had begun. But now it was up and his books, his diaries and his specimens were neatly laid out on the ground sheet beside the duck-down sleeping bag he had kept from his climbing days as an undergraduate. The familiar lent a sense of closeness, as he checked everything over with the torch. A small green canvas bag held his digging tools, the miniature spade and a Botanist's trowel for uprooting specimens. A side pocket, with his maps in, bulged onto one side of the tent which flapped as the cool night breeze turned at the Pomos cliff top and rolled back down the side of the mountain.

"Strange!" he thought, as he surveyed the few items which made up his professional world. "Strange how academia promotes a complicated life style where there aren't enough hours in the day to write the papers and deal with the Publishers and keep up a gruelling lecture schedule. Yet here I am in a tent on a hillside in a remote part of the Akamas National Park with a trowel and a gardener's spade looking for a needle in a haystack." He reminded himself of the lesson he had learnt in Cyprus. "It's the quality of life whilst you're looking that counts. It's the journey not the destination."

He thought also of Brasenose, Oxford with its spacious quads, its medieval gargoyles, the smells of the evening meal emerging from the buttery, the rich brandies and ports emptied at the top table where he had presided some evenings when the Warden was away. He really had to chuckle. The posturing amidst the trappings of privilege was a theatrical ruse that scholarly people often played upon themselves to convince themselves they were living safely tucked away from the 'nasties' of life that sometimes News at Ten displayed on the Senior Common Room T.V. screen during sherry receptions.

Oxford's sedate and archaic rituals, he mused, were there to dazzle undergraduates and American and Japanese tourists; make them feel they were in some kind of intellectual heaven; offer young hopefuls degrees of which none would question the validity.

Sampson got up to take his night stroll and picking his way up though brushwood listened to the dogs howling over the valleys sending their ghostly messages from village to village. He'd slept well these last two nights—and without the aid of even a light dose of sleeping tablets. He felt he should always reach into his pocket for them but knew that now he'd done without them intermittently over the last three months he would probably never look back. Undiga was there in support—she'd managed to drop him a note and told him how she'd got the week off work in July so that she could come to watch him in the 'Tempest' at Kourion.

He found a broad flat area where he could gaze out over the Mediterranean and breath in the sensuous night. He felt that she was beside him and that they would lie here on the cliff top the whole night through only to be awoken by the tinkle of the goatbells as they passed below at dawn.

He could see one single fishing vessel below in the bay, the red lantern hanging in the windless night at the front of the boat to attract the fish. The rest was complete calm, the surface of the water resembling a large ice-skating rink reflecting the moon.

Such was the stillness that he plainly heard the giant splash as the anchor or other weight went off the boat into the water. Then a moment or two passed and he saw the figure of the fisherman moving about the boat. Sampson fancied he heard the air to "Wild Mountain Thyme", a ballad that was a favourite of his, but he shook himself and turned back to the path he had taken. "Must be some local tune that sounds a little bit like the Scottish song!" he said to himself. "Cypriot businessmen and bar owners are not bad at English but fishermen wouldn't know that tune!"

The tall trireme named '*Odysseas*' had been made in the Piraeus docks in 430BC and its maiden journey, according to the Greek historians, had been to Paphos. Captain Achilleos had known his route. He had been doing the trip for three years and was familiar with the sand-banks and shoals that lay between Rhodos and the Hellenic centres of Asia Minor. Once through this, he knew it would be easy sailing past Mikros Nesos and directly across to Paphos harbour.

The Meltemi, that celebrated Mediterranean wind, had been on their back and had given them great speed. Captain Achilleos felt comfortable that his cargo was safe, a beautiful new statue of Aphrodite fashioned in stone by Praxiteles, at that time famous throughout the Hellenic world because of his unsurpassable statue of Hermes installed at Olympia. The marble Goddess had been loaded at Argos under the supervision of the great sculptor himself. He had been sure, too, that the Goddess would lead them safely to their destination, since that was the home of her birth and a place where her temples and altars dominated the slopes of Troodos where a second Mt. Olympus harboured Gods as ancient as those of Delphi and Achaea.

As he scanned the seas ahead, he had prayed: "Oh great winds of Meltemi and Notos and you, the gods and goddesses of mountain and journey who help to control their path, send us safely today to Paphos shores. Aphrodite, Goddess of Love, I will worship at your altar tomorrow. I will bring the flowers and incense that melt your heart and I will carry to you a representation of your beauty carved by our great Praxiteles."

Once though the straits, the trireme's sails puffed out and he had the ten stout sailors from Argos pull in the sheets tight, so that he could get close to the wind. Speed picked up and the Goddess was racing home across the closing stretch of the Eastern Mesogeia. The slaves in the galley would have little to do now. All was in the hands of the Gods.

Jan approached the sloping statue. It lay looking up half-embedded in the muddy sand. The deep eddy tides had turned sand and deposits over it so much that, as he touched it with his thickly padded gloves, the sharp ends of barnacles prodded through. He turned the dive-torch up its spiky torso to look at the face. Amazingly, the large rounded eyes, favoured for goddesses in ancient Greece, stared back at him. He could make out the tresses of her hair tried neatly with a ribbon around the brow, a few curls allowing themselves to hang temptingly down over the forehead. Quickly, he assessed that the head had lain for a long time protected somewhere, perhaps lodged under a rock whilst the rest of the body, stretched in its classical shroud, had lain open to the ravages of the salty sea. He took the end of the rope he had brought down with him and attempted to lift the head to wrap it underneath. Lead jars lay toppled on their sides; handles of urns peered from the muddy bottom. He tied the knot, a double bowline, and, rising a little from the bottom, tugged on the rope to alert Jock.

As Jan descended to bottom again he felt a snag on his main breathing hose. A quick attack of panic grasped him. He turned to look. A sharp razor-like edge of a barnacle had sheared his main hose, as he had brushed past the statue. The bubbles were springing out of the neat slit it had made. He grappled to put the spare on, releasing a safety catch as he pushed it to his mouth and started to breath. He sucked for the air and oxygen but it was slow to arrive.

He could see that clearly Jock had felt the tug up top, as the statue was being pulled upright and now was rising. But the urgency for Jan was to get his air coming through clean. Although the water was muddied from the rising Goddess, he could make out a clip, that should have been holding the fresh hose on to the back of the tank cylinders, lying to his left on the seabed.

As soon as Jock had registered that the rope was in place, he put the winch immediately on to automatic. As the winch took the load, it fell back a little before locking again.

How could he have known, up top, that a slight release of pressure on the winch was enough to let the full weight of Aphrodite come down on Jan as he stumbled looking for the clip? How could he know the outcome of the rolling out of the chain? The base of the statue ripped the rubber diving cap off Jan's head, sliced and cracked his skull and left him bleeding on the site of the ancient wreck.

Jock was giddy with expectation. The one and a half bottles of Scotch he had emptied, in the course of that afternoon and evening, made him feel capable and strong as he watched the boat keel to its port side to balance the workload the winch was supporting. The statue was now on its way up and, as the chain revolved, he sang: 'Over the sea to Skye' . . .

"speed Bonnie boat like a bird on the wind . . . over the sea to . . ." His last word in the line was now interrupted by a noisy hiccup. The 15 year old single malt was taking its toll. He rolled his frame over from the winch to starboard, from where his partner had descended twenty five minutes before. Despite his hazy state, he knew that Jan should soon surface. He would, for that depth of dive, have had to stop twice to decompress, once at forty feet depth; again at twenty feet. But those halts would only have been for ten minutes then for five, in that order.

They needed each other in their new found success. Jan looked after the European connections in Amsterdam. Jock did the London and New York end of business.

"C'mon, Jan laddie. We've done a gud job so far. Get yerself up here and let's get this lady out of here."

As he spoke, the lady he referred to quite suddenly appeared at his side. He just looked up and in the red glow of the Gri Gri lantern saw her bird like eyes coming vengefully for him as she swung free of the waves and toppled towards the winch. He pushed the button. All noise stopped. She hung suspended over the boat, the rope around her neck. She looked, for all the world, the part of a murderess who'd been left to hang, publicly exposed after her execution.

Only the crickets could be heard and a very soft wash of the foam, as it hit the rocks by the beach. He gaped, with awe, as he realised just how beautiful the marble representation was, how ancient, how important to Cyprus she must be.

John Sampson had returned to the tent and, by the light of the bush lamp, was ticking off the specimens he had been able to sight and collect from the 'Rare Flowers of the Eastern Mediterranean'. Although, after his nine months stay, he could count one hundred and four spotted with samples taken, another twelve which interested him lay undiscovered. They were probably all around him, in these olive groves, he mused, as he blew out the lamp and settled in for the night. Perhaps they hid a little further up by the ridge where they lived nourished on the sea-breezes from the bay of Pomos and hardened by the volcanic deposits of ash which had been spewed up from the bowels of mother earth millions of years ago. No longer, he knew, would he need to reach for the

Kostas Tzelalis 2013

sleeping tablets which had been "the crutch through stormy times," as his GP in Oxford had described them.

With the healing scent of Oleander flower in his nose, he fell quietly asleep.

Captain Achilleos took a draught of the dark Daphne wine that was offered to him by his chief sailor, Thymios, who hailed from Nafplion, near Argos. The captain had been at the steering oar for a good four hours and was tiring. "Let me help you," said Thymios. "Go below and rest. I will hold the oar stick for the next hour."

"That will be very fine" said Achilleos, knowing that he should refresh himself, check the galley slaves and mark in his position below deck. "But we are approaching Cyprus and will soon need to turn in order to follow the coast from Pomos Point down to Latchi and Paphos. When you first see the white cliff tops of the promontory, you need to turn".

"Very good," replied the first mate. "I'll do that master".

It was twenty minutes later that Thymios spotted, to his right, the high chalky cliffs. They were not those of Pomos, as he thought. They were the luring cliffs of Kokkina Point near Pyrgos. He turned right to head towards them, locked his keel on to the stout oak holding-beam and ran down to alert his captain. When Captain Achilleos came back up, he knew he was off course but the last thing he wanted was to arrive at the top of the island beyond Pyrgos because the two winds combined, those coming off the land masses of Asia Minor above Cyprus and those of the island itself, could turn ships around, upend them, sink them.

The Meltemi blew him fast and hard towards the bay. If he could keep on course now, all would be well. He suddenly remembered that, throughout all the journey, he had prayed to Aphrodite herself and to the Gods of Wind and, in passing only, had made mention of the great God of the Sea, Poseidon. All Greek sailors knew to pray to him as Protector of Ships, but he had been taken in by the importance of his task, conveying such a fine statue to Paphos itself. He had forgotten to ask Poseidon to watch over them as he had left port.

Then he saw the whirling black spout, spinning along the waves and blowing up dust as it touched the land. He knew in that moment that

Poseidon must have argued with Aphrodite and the *Odysseas* was now caught up in a violent tiff between them. His mother had told him, as a child, how stormy the relationship was between the Goddess, who was born and delivered on the white tops of the waves at Paphos, and that God that all Greeks feared, Poseidon of the deep.

Jock had paused to stare with admiration at his prize. She swung freely from the chain, swivelling her body as though looking for admiration but, each time her face stopped in front of him, a bitter expression seemed to mark her face, and her dissatisfaction appeared to be highlighted by the blood-red arc of the kri kri fishing light, hanging at the end of the boat, being reflected upwards upon her.

Despite his awe, he began to fear for his partner's safety. Something had gone wrong. If he'd got the bends at only fifty feet or so he could still be saved, if, that is, he remembered his breathing exercises. He needed his partner. Nobody else could be trusted to help him dispose of the Goddess.

'I know! I know what I'll do, Jan! While you are taking your time getting up here, I'll take this lady down and make her comfortable in the boat. How about that"

Jock made his way over to where the crane was supporting the chain that went through the pulley. This fell to where it surrounded her neck in a double tie, half chain and half rope. Just a touch of his palm, pushed gently against her folds on the marble image, was enough to tell him there was a tremendous weight on the pulley and the springs of the crane.

He reached up to pull the pulley cage down, so he could rest the bottom of the statue on the boat. He released the catch at the head of the mini crane and she dropped quickly. The chain, since it was supporting a swivelling statue, wrapped itself suddenly round and round his upraised hand and before he knew about it cut deep into his hand. Tugging his arm and hand away, he looked at them in deep disbelief. It was enough to sober him. The sharp edge of the chain had swathed right through his hand and, although it was still partially suspended from his wrist, it hung there, the fingers lifeless and disconnected from the main nerve ends. Blood spouted everywhere. He grabbed a cloth and attempted to stem the flow but one of his minor arteries was gushing fast and he suddenly felt a faint coming over him.

Blacking out for Jock was like falling over; falling when ye'd had too much at New Year. The eyes roll; ye try to say *"I'll have another wee one."* Then, before anyone could pour him one, or before he could even help himself to the bottle, he just collapsed into a deep and dark sleep. The last thing he remembered was the lady slowly descending to the deck to lie beside him, in what had now become the first stirrings of twilight on Pomos bay.

The spout came at the *Odysseas* as only a God in temper could, sweeping the mainsail in its path, ripping it asunder, cracking the booms that came off the main mast. The strong lads of Argos cowered like ants on the deck of the ship.

"Oimai. Oimai," they cried.

Achilleos pulled two of them up from the deck and made them bring the Goddess up from below.

"She'll save us," he roared.

The two would try that or anything at this moment. They needed the strength that an almighty could offer. In five minutes she was up. Achilleos held her, touching her rounded marble folds and whispered: "Goddess, this is your Island! You wish to get one day to Paphos—save yourself!"

As he held her, the twisting nightmare hauled the trireme towards Pomos. The water spout needed to hit land again to gather more strength from the heat of the earth itself.

When, three minutes later, the *Odysseas* went down, the Captain still held, in tight embrace, his Goddess. All but one of the men from Argos perished that day, as the eddy sucked them down. Only Thymios escaped, swept into shore with the spliced boom that had been within hand's reach, as he toppled overboard.

Thymios returned to Greece and told his story to the early Athenian historian who recorded the incident, as an example of the dangers Greek sailors underwent during the years of Athenian expansion.

When Sampson, tent on back, refreshed with good sleep and light of foot, looked out over the bay at seven on the last morning of his three day field trip, he had a good view directly down on to the boat. The statue stared up at him. He took out his binoculars for a closer inspection. It was unmistakably Aphrodite. Despite being covered with barnacles, her regal countenance and her braided hair announced her identity. Adjusting the lenses and moving them to left and right he could make out something— it looked like a body with a cap and a sea jacket hiding the face, lying to the right side of the statue's broad frame.

"What on earth has happened here?" he whispered to himself

Sampson ran to descend the steep track that led to the beach. Normally, he refreshed himself in the sea first thing in the morning anyway, so he decided to swim out to the small fishing vessel and investigate. He was able to get out there in under ten minutes and, pulling himself over the side, the scene that greeted him was most bizarre. A goddess on her back with a rope around her neck, two whiskey bottles and a winch. The signs of diving preparations; the kri-kri lantern still lit though there had been already an hour of daylight; but most of all what looked like a lifeless form of a man. Part of the face, now exposed, looked ashen but not exactly lifeless as the closed eyelids still flickered as though reacting to a bad dream.

As he pieced together the noises of the night before and the fact that here was his former adversary and tormentor, in form of stone, gazing up at him from an unmanned boat, he knew he could not handle this situation alone. He turned immediately to swim back the two hundred metres to shore. He would get back as quickly as possible to the car, then dash on to contact the coast guard through the police post at Pyrgos.

A week later, the "Cyprus Mail" reported how one body had been brought up by an Air-Sea Rescue team, sent in from the British base at Akrotiri. The drowned man had been lodged under rocks for some days, his weight belt still dragging him down, until a new tide had washed his remains a kilometre up the coast from where their boat had been found. A second man, found in the boat, had, against all odds, recovered consciousness after two days in intensive care. He had had to have his hand amputated but was now well enough to help police and coastguard with their enquiries

Aphrodite had found her way to the Paphos Museum. The statue was undergoing special cleaning treatment and Kyrios Nicolaides, the curator, was hailing the find as the most important for a century.

Sampson, reading the newspaper report in the weekend edition of the Cyprus Mail in his usual corner of the taverna at Tremithousa, reflected how he'd been allowed to witness Aphrodite's deft powers yet again. He suspected he was now no longer a target, so long as he protected her environment and tread wary of her moods. But, just when he was beginning to normalize his sleep patterns and the nightmares, usually figuring representations of the Goddess, were beginning to recede, here suddenly was a more concrete reminder that this island and the sea that surrounded it were most definitely her territory.

She would exact a terrible revenge on those that transgressed. The irony of the choice of execution tool had not escaped Sampson. She had used the very chain, the one that they were using to kidnap her from her domain, to reverse their fortune. She had used their own winch to kill one and maim the other.

Episode 9

Stavros Tis Stokkas

John was surprised by the way the sudden opening in the dense pine forest provided an abrupt break from the continuous sway of green, which swept down from this high point to carpet the Troodos mountains in verdant majesty. He was not surprised, however, to see only a small group of cabins standing side by side at the opposite end of the clearing. He had already been apprised about the lay of the land by Margo. Stavros tis Stokkas was not a village nor was it a hamlet of any sort. It was too high, too remote, too inaccessible. Workers of the Cyprus Forestry Commission took turns to spend a fortnight at a time up there, on the highest summit in the range, to watch out for fires from the observation post nearby and to feed and guard the wild moufflons which were fenced into a clearance to protect their numbers.

Five simple huts housed the forestry workers. Smoke from the fires that warmed them could always be seen from the villages of the foothills of the Paphos Mountains. Now, in early April, having managed to rent out one of the huts, John needed a fire. The nights, in contrast with the 32 degrees daytime temperature, had turned cold.

It was approaching midnight. Sampson lay on the small wooden frame that served as a bed in one of those huts, his eyes fixed on page forty six of 'Flowers of Cyprus' upon which was displayed a well-thumbed pen and ink drawing of *the Akamas Centaury*. This tiny inoffensive specimen was endemic to Cyprus; it grew nowhere else in the world. He reflected upon the geological history of the island. Volcanic eruption had, according to the experts in that field, hurled the land masses up from their attachments to North Africa, spilling the spewed up molten magma and basaltic materials onto the lime that was already embedded there and finally topping the giant dollop of earth with what is termed the 'nappe,' a topping mix of limestone and granite crust. At this very moment he was lying at the apex of that pile, around fifteen million years on. Vegetation which had died out elsewhere had been locked in to the island just as, he supposed, certain species of lemur had been preserved uniquely for Madagascar when, eons ago, that island had slipped away from the African continent into the Indian Ocean.

Now he gazed at this botanical gem, so much sought after by a few professors like himself who, he felt, were themselves in danger of becoming rare species. Very likely, he thought, the pen and ink drawings would die out with people like himself. Computerized images had been the order of the day for so many years now. In seconds you could search out an assimilation, or a scanned photograph, of a very rare flower on the internet. No more loving sketches by botanists who might bring a picnic along and spend long days in remote areas with pens and watercolours.

Although he thought of himself as youthful at heart, in fact, these days so rejuvenated he imagined Undiga and Cyprus had given him a new lease of life, he regretted the passing of an era in which the botanist could, if he desired, be in communion with the natural settings for his studies.

The gray hardback and slightly dog-eared book which had become for him a twin source of learning, a map of his own journey of rediscovery and a chart of his progress in unearthing some of the true treasures of Cyprus, fell gently from his hand. The eyes closed and as they did so the flower blossomed large in the thalamus of his mind, there at the threshold of dream. The golden yellow tips and mauve-purple colours of the *Centaury* weaved prints which changed to moving images. Quickly, effortlessly, he turned into a Gandalph figure magically controlling the forms which appeared and disappeared before him. Space and time no longer restrained him.

He is flying high and free and his massive wingspan casts an even larger shadow over the Akamas cliffs as he soars in, from God knows where, to Cyprus. As an eagle might, he feels the warm blasts of air, created by the heat of the island landmass, lift him. He raises his head to guide himself up the ascent of wooded Troodos and a whoosh of air whistles through the tilted wings. He sets his direction by the sun which lies, a great circle of illumination and power, crowning Mt Olympos at the highest point of the island's mountainous bulk.

As he approaches the holy sanctuary of Olympos, the image changes to Aphrodite herself, her hair braided at the temples in classic greek style, the rest of her ringlets flowing free. She gives orders to her legions to pursue the invader who has breached her borders without permission. An army of furies are dispatched. She lifts her beautiful but cold green eyes to the sun and speaks. In the haze of sleep, Sampson cannot make out her words. He is struggling to grasp them, for she is warning him of something.

In a flash her face changes to that of Undiga. The hair has changed from dark to blonde and is hanging free, eyes of sparkling blue and an invitation, half sexual, half motherly, as she proudly offers him her breast, standing proud against the northern fairness of her rounded contours.

The eagle changes to the triangular shape of a hang glider, soaring over the down-slopes of Troodos. He is aware of the blue and gold craft, at first sky-gliding and slow, then falling rapidly into the thick pine forests of Troodos. The trees come up at him at an extraordinary pace, earth swallowing sky.

He physically felt the frisson that moved quickly through his left shoulder and into the muscles around the heart as he awoke, aware that his throat was parched. He reached for the water in the jug that sat on the rough-hewn bedside table. Drinking thirstily, he wondered why such a vivid dream had returned to him after four months of freedom from his nightmares. When his relationship with Undiga had begun in late September of last year, the recurrent haunting, always featuring Aphrodite, each time in a different mythic setting, had gradually subsided and, in January of this year, he had believed it had disappeared.

He put on the light and took his 'Flowers of Cyprus' from the floor. He would need half an hour now to find his sleep again, searching the pages for such calming prints as Cyprus Iris and the Sage—leaved flower commonly known as the Rock Rose. These images, he knew, would submerge those others of feathers and wings that lay pinned to the treetops.

The head forester, Kypros, woke him brusquely by pushing the jaded and creaking wooden frame of the door ajar. It had not been locked. Sampson could not remember ever having locked his door in Cyprus. The dark-skinned forester placed the scented mountain herbal tea and toast on the table.

"*Ella koumbare*, you told me to wake you . . . its six. I'll have the jeep ready in ten minutes to take you over to Daskarou. You'll find these film crews don't wait. They want to catch the morning mist rising over the pines and the movements of the animals in their morning migration." Kypros spoke English with an Australian accent, the 'i' in migration sounding like 'oy' and the 'gra' like 'grai'. He'd explained over the *raki* last night how he had studied Forestry at Ku-Ring-Gai national Park which skirted the northern boundaries of the city of Sydney. He had worked there for five years before coming back to take up the position of Head Forester at Stavros.

Sampson bit into the soft white cheese called *anari*, which topped the toast, making a mental note to take out and reread the guideline questions sent out from London. This was camera day, he retold himself as he stepped out of the door, pulling on a brown, all-weather, coat and a green cap. Although he had worked out a script that answered the rather matter-of-fact questions, asking him to name the rarer flowers and say a few words on each, he had been made aware that it was how he looked in front of the camera that was most important. If he tripped on words they could be dubbed in later. Margo had emailed through to the Cypriot RIK TV office, letting them and him know all relevant details, since Channel 4 would be using some of their archive material and asking them to supply a local cameraman and two soundmen.

Margo would be here today too. She had flown into Paphos last night. He wondered whether she'd find any changes in him. As for her, he imagined she would be just her buoyant normal self. She represented the other kind of friendship that he needed. Shared interests and a certain professional dynamism now united them.

He passed the enclosure where the moufflons (he knew the Greek translation as *agrina)* were kept. One large male trotted protectively around the smaller, more petite, females. Then, on impulse, nose in the air, the male rushed at the fence and leapt two yards off the ground, landing precisely on a tiny circle of ground beside the water bucket. The agility of these animals and their precision never ceased to amaze him.

Kypros called him to the landrover parked on the other side of the enclosure. He hurried over to take his seat for the steep ride up to Daskarou.

"I see the *palekari* is showing off to you then," the Cypriot said, as they pulled out through the pines to a sign pointing up to Daskarou-Panolimbos.

"What do you mean *palekari*?" John asked. He was always ready to learn a new word.

"*Palekari* is usually what we call a strong man, a warrior. But here we use it to describe that male deer-goat you've just been watching. You know the females that are out in the wild come up to the perimeter fence every night to parade for him? One night he jumped the twelve foot fence and took off with his chosen mate. We recaptured both of them and now keep the happy pair together. Matter of fact they're both being shipped to Greece shortly as a wedding present for the President's daughter."

The landrover sent thick clouds of dust streaming out from its skirts as it snaked up the twisting track to Daskarou. John pencilled over his prepared notes, putting in accentuation marks where he would put some sort of emphasis into what promised to be a fairly dull lecture. The latin names rolled off the tongue as they had done for 18 years in the busy Oxford lecture rooms.

"Cyclamen Cyprium, found only in Cyprus at heights of 3000 feet above sea level, it's distinctive white heart opens out to bright yellow inner leaves when darkness falls." Sampson read the piece dispassionately to himself, before slipping the colour print that he had of it behind the sheet of paper and attaching the two with a paper clip. Later, he could hold the print up for the camera and read his notes whilst the lens provided a close up of the details. Not that he needed to read his lines. The facts had been imprinted on his memory a long time ago when he had been doing his doctoral thesis and had never been allowed to slip away since he had regularly lectured or written papers on them.

The morning mists were clearing from the pine clad peaks where the sun touched them first. Different views of Olympos and the higher mountains came into view as the angle changed with each turn in the road. The interior of Cyprus displayed an aspect of the surreal on such a morning. Not a hint of any industrial activity and the green vegetation releasing only natural chemicals into the clean air.

Sampson, as consultant botanist to the director, had been able to select a spot for filming where, since it was located at 3800 feet above sea level and due to the purity of the air and the water streaming out from the many waterfalls, the wild endemic orchids of Cyprus could be seen growing lush at the side of the dirt track road that led to the fire observation post.

More agrina, running free, and the occasional snake, startled by the noisy rumble of the landrover's approach, could be seen gliding into the deep forests. The many bends, folded into the route because of the severity of the climb, provided an element of surprise every few minutes.

"Look! There's the Cyprus Woodsinger!" said Kypros as they upset a flock of long tailed black and white birds from a thicket of pine gorse near the road. "That's the one you used to see on the old Cyprus 20 cent coin, or as the Cypriots call it the *shillinga*. That's before this new-fangled euro took over! That bird has the most beautiful song. Legend has it that Aphrodite lures her love victims into these mountains using that song"

At the mention of Aphrodite, John noticed how his muscles had tightened and he sought to busy himself with the notes.

'*Barlia Robertiano*, also known as the giant Orchid, the rarest of the family of orchids, is known only at two sites in the world both of which are found high in the Cyprus mountains.' He penciled in the next bit. 'One of those places is here at Daskarou where the lush vegetation and nearby mountain streams provide the moisture it requires.' Then he added his own stage direction:

'Sampson points to landscape behind'

He also knew that *Alyssum Troodi*, of which there were splendid examples at Daskarou, could not be left out. The Latin and the description rolled from his pencil onto the paper 'sometimes called Cyprus Cruciferae, Alysssum Troodi, relative of Alyssum Strigosum and Alyssum Alpinum found at high altitude. Identified by Steadman 1926 in the upper reaches of the Troodos range'.

Then the pencil snapped.

"Damn. Damn it!" exploded Sampson

"What's up Professor?" asked his driver.

"Oh I don't know. These flowers are my life and just the sight of them growing wild gives me real pleasure but this film thing . . . . I mean what do I do . . . . rattle off all these names and hold up the pictures? Now the pencil's snapped on me."

"I'm sure you will be all right when you get started into it," said the Cypriot, "It's probably all just nerves"

Sampson turned his attention to ordering the photographs and marking them one to eight. Just as he was doing this, however, the landrover came up to a straight stretch of road, at the end of which Sampson could see a flurry of activity. They were at the location.

Then as the vehicle drew up at the cul de sac where the small round hut, which served as Cyprus' highest fire-lookout post, was positioned, John immediately caught sight of Margo, her red hair markedly visible in the throng of dark Cypriot cameramen and assistants. She held, fixed on her face, that broad healthy smile that had almost ensnared him nine months before at the Taverna. Well, yes, he remembered, to be truthful it *had* captivated him, although he hadn't been quite ready to take things further. He got out of the jeep, went over to her and kissed her warmly on both cheeks.

"Welcome John. You look great. You've put on some weight"

"Margo, marvellous to see you again. If I look great then I certainly don't feel it!"

"What's up, John? Nervous?"

"To tell you the truth Margo, yes. Very! I received all your instructions about writing down the names of flowers you can film in this spot and a brief description of them and all that stuff. Yet, when I tried to put it all together, it was just too much like a list. There is no heart in it. Know what I mean?"

"Just relax, John. All we need are the correct genus and species and a little spiel on each—then we want to see your famous face fronting it. Later we'll film, acting on your advice, some of the flowers *in situ* and eventually we'll collage it all into a half hour documentary. You can also make mistakes you know—we'll just make new takes. Now come and meet the director. He's very flexible and has left this particular episode of 'Forgotten Treasures of Cyprus' to me and yourself to work out."

Suddenly the pressure seemed to wane a little and after John had been with the director for his ten minute briefing, during which he was taught how to look directly into the camera like a true anchorman, he was even beginning to look forward to this experience. Flexibility, he said to himself, that is the name of the game here.

Emotion rang out in his voice. Margo had to step forward to better catch the expression on his face and to savour the choice expression that a visibly transformed John Sampson was pouring forth for the camera. It had been but half an hour since he had arrived, worried and nervous. Yet here he was giving what Margo thought was an exceptional performance. It was as though he had been doing this all his life, she mused. He had walked back to the hedge at the edge of the dirt track and, carefully holding the stem of a large orchid which had red spots daubed on its silky yellow petals, he was talking directly into the camera:

"This is one of the rarest flowers in the world and it grows here in one of the most rarified atmospheres in the world where the ancient Greeks believed the Gods resided. Behind us here is Mount Olympos, the namesake of the famous mountain in Greece where the Gods of Homer held sway over mortal matters."

Margo watched the camera pan out away from John to take in the awesome sight of the peak of Mt Olympos rising out of the mist. Then the cameraman centred on the flower.

"In nine months I myself have seen how these precious surviving treasures can make a person come alive. Anyone who feels jaded with the modern cities of Europe should come to Cyprus and walk the high paths of these mountains where, against all the odds, flowers like this orchid have survived for millions of years. And if one were to ask why, then one might, as I have done, feel the heady mixture of the geology and the mythology of the island where Aphrodite, goddess of fertility and beauty, began her rule when Homer introduced her to the world 2, 900 years ago. When you hear the whisper of Homer's words about her, as you walk by her ancient temples in the area of Paphos, you could be forgiven for believing she still protects her symbols of beauty and procreation."

"Well!" thought Margo. "This is certainly different. But I think I like what he is getting at. Above all he sounds sincere. He feels what he is talking about. The TV audience will go for this I think!"

Sampson moved over to his left and stepped a little further back into the shrubbery, so that he could reach up to the upper leaves of a green bush on which grew small white buds.

"You, like me, need to smell the freshness of this tiny gem to really appreciate it." Here John pulled a bud towards his nose and inhaled what he intimated to be like nectar. "This is the Cyprus snowdrop which requires the most balanced ecological conditions. On the other hand you may never get to smell this or another seventy specimens on the RED Endangered list made out by the EU, if the bulldozers, that are operating all over this island to build hotels and holiday villages and golf courses, ever reach this area"

"Good," reflected Margo. "He's making a stance on behalf of protecting the environment. That goes down very well with the general public these days." But, more than anything, Margo marvelled at the ease he displayed in front of the camera and wondered whether this was the same person she had gone out with, at the time of his early searches for rare flowers in Akamas. She remembered her initial interest in him when she had met him at the taverna in Tremithousa and then she recalled how she had quickly realized that, somehow, he was carrying a lot of baggage from his past. As lovers, it had not worked out but, as she caught herself beaming with pride in him, she thought that he might now be more amenable to having another try.

For twenty minutes John walked the length of the foliage that skirted the track. Sometimes he held up a pen and ink drawing of a certain species to the camera, sometimes he talked, gesturing widely, and occasionally he was able to point out a plant or a flower from the range that grew along that single stretch.

Margo sensed when he was about to complete, for he had walked slowly forward toward the camera with, as the director had taught him, his eyes firmly fixed on the focus lens. She could see the director and other assistants gather behind the camera, an element of expectancy stamped on their faces as though they were involved in a drama, not just another documentary. John Sampson needed no notes or prompting. He gave a final statement:

"And I believe that, in a sense, the Greeks were right to have a goddess of the wood and a god of the river. They acted as protectors. People were frightened to harm nature because they were frightened of upsetting the gods. The chief deity of this island, Aphrodite, still protects these rare examples of a world of beauty but she protects them, as she protects all the treasures of this island, through spokespeople. I am very proud to have become, via a certain baptism of fire, such a spokesperson and to have had the opportunity to show you today these wonderful specimens in their natural setting."

"Cut it there!" the director called out. He went up to the botanist and shook his hand. "Well, it was very different from a 'Gardener's World' type broadcast, John, but we should be able to use some of that. Margo will give you the schedule for our other meetings this week. I think you have already worked out locations, mainly in the Akamas area, is that not so?"

"Yes we've agreed on three places for filming. But there's no talking to camera in those places, is there?"

"No. I think we just need to get film of perhaps ten more species and, if necessary, we'll get you to voice over their names in a studio later. So that's it, John. Thanks a lot. Personally I really enjoyed what you had to say today. We'll have to convince the executive producers now that the TV audiences will lap it up."

Everything had been packed into the back of Margo's four wheel drive. Kypros was going back down alone and John had accepted an invitation from Margo for ouzo and mezze by the seaside, down at Limassol. They descended by a different route to the one John had come up on, winding down long dusty tracks through the pine forest in the direction of Troodos village from which they would rapidly drop down to the coastal plain where Limassol sprawled. That city was, thought John, a perfect example of the 'bulldozer country' he had spoken of in his camera speech. A long line of hotels and bars, it was a favourite spot for the young revellers who came to Cyprus every year in their millions, tourists looking for aphrodisiac qualities in the island that was always marketed as Aphrodite's island.

Margo told him on the way down that he seemed to have changed since she had spent that week, nine months before, with him. He appeared to her confident and expressive. She said she liked his new image. Was he aware that he had changed? He found himself explaining to her that there was someone who had played an important role in a kind of personal inner healing process. Yes, he was aware that a kind of catharsis had taken place and overtaken him as he had got to know Undiga. He told her also of the strange perceptions he had that, in dream and in daytime reality, Aphrodite or possibly, he admitted, what Aphrodite stood for, was imparting a message to him.

Margo remembered him referring to Aphrodite that first night she had met him in Tremithousa. She had become aware, in the following week when she accompanied him on his quests for flowers, that here was a man almost haunted by a dissatisfaction with his past and by disturbing dreams in which the figure of Aphrodite, in different guises, played a major role. She couldn't help feel a twinge of regret and jealousy, though, when John related how close he had got to Undiga. "How come Undiga could do what she herself hadn't?" she asked herself.

But she listened with intent to John's tales of the sea change at Drepanum that almost killed both him and Undiga. Then there was the story of the murder of Mrs Dolly from the International School. She felt the drama, too, as he told how his nightmares had somehow returned, after originally thinking he could deal with them. Only a month ago he had a sharp reminder of the mysterious power at work when the two divers trying to recover and steal an ancient statue of the Goddess had been maimed or killed in the quiet night waters off Pomos bay. Coincidences he told her—of course coincidence—and also a coincidence that he, John Sampson, had found the boat next morning and had actually heard the splash of one diver entering the water. Somehow he had witnessed too many coincidences in Cyprus, in a very short period of time.

As they approached Limassol, Margo noticed John staring out to the sky above the sea that lay off the city.

"What are you looking at, John?" she said.

Silence and still he stared.

"Something interesting up there?"

"Well, it's another of those coincidences," he said. "Those hang gliders you can see, coming down off the Troodos and panning out over the bay, they played a part in my latest dream"

"Well, that's not too farfetched. You see them all over the island at every resort. People will dream about them!"

"That's true. It's just that my dream featured the Cyprus rare orchids and then they turned into a hang glider. Then today, consecutively, I am in close contact with both."

"I think you are putting too much meaning into all these dreams and events John. You are a botanist! You see pictures of Orchids everywhere. You live in Cyprus. You see hang gliders often enough. The events govern the dream not the other way round"

"Yes, Margo, well I just hope they don't fly too close to the sun that's all."

Margo was pulling the car up at an *ouzerio* on the Limassol front. As she got out and walked ahead of him into the cafe, she wondered what on earth could have given rise to that last remark.

John, meanwhile, followed her in, musing to himself that, coincidence or not, he no longer felt bewildered or mystified. He had accepted Cyprus on its own terms now and, having broadcast to the world a message that seemed to have been weighing on him ever since he had arrived, he now felt utterly relieved. It was as though, after a long period of strife, a truce had been struck with the protecting deity on this island and new terms of conduct were now in operation.

EPISODE 10

Fontana Amorosa

Even as he watched the Scandinavian Airways jet flying over the bay on its approach to the small airport of Paphos, John Sampson, out at sea on a 38 foot yacht with his Cypriot friends Andreas and Michaelis, could not be sure that Undiga was on it. She was not the best of letter writers, plus he had no access to emails or the internet in the mountains and all he was going on was the cryptic message sent one week ago on the back of a postcard portraying the city hall in Oslo; 'Paphos 2nd. Bergen flight.'

Recently, with the arrival of the fine early summer weather, he increasingly found the opportunity to get out on his friends' boat and feel those eastern Mediterranean winds lift and ease the sails so quickly that, at any one moment, the boat could be cutting the water at a slightly terrifying angle, then, ten or fifteen minutes later, the winds would drop and leave them 'in irons,' going nowhere. In the latter case, they would simply lie back and drift or start the motor and putter off round the coast. Such contrasts and the healing touches of summer breezes upon his tanning body, as he manoeuvred around the deck of *Priest Apollo* learning the use of the rigging, tightening and loosening the sail ropes on the winches, occasionally taking up position at the navsat or practicing his chartwork, had put him in fine spirits. He had also been able to work up to getting his day skipper licence and could now borrow the boat for a day at a time.

This feeling of well-being was all the more underlined when Sampson compared his present existence with the harrowing experiences of his first months in Cyprus. For one thing, his sleep was no longer punctuated by vivid dreams in which the main haunting figure would be Aphrodite, the island's patron goddess. She had returned less and less frequently, the last time having been the night before he delivered his speech to the cameras for the Channel 4 documentary, and now it was as though he had rid himself completely of the ghost that had pursued him. Yet still, as he looked up at the aeroplane, the daily flight in from Norway, there was the niggling belief that all would not go well, that somehow he didn't deserve this beautiful girl. Maybe she had changed her mind anyway. She wouldn't be on the flight. He recognized ghosts of a different nature lurking deep in his subconscious.

He pushed any dark thoughts out of his mind for the present and busied himself with preparations for turning the boat towards the shore. He forced himself to think positively and constructively. Undiga, the catalyst to his remarkable recovery over the last ten months, was sure to be arriving in Cyprus on that very jet he could see making its approach over the bay, after a three and a half hour direct flight from Oslo to Paphos. That had to be good news.

Today he would surprise her by whisking her and her baggage onto the yacht and navigating round to *Fontana Amorosa* for a picnic lunch on the coral lagoon. All he and his friends had to do now was to turn back to the small quay, which lay just half a mile south of the airstrip. Andreas had parked his car there at the fish restaurant and a short ride, through the pines that lined the coastline at this point, would mean that, in something like twenty minutes from the moment they turned for shore, John would be at the airport.

Approaching the land, the depth of the water dropped rapidly, the crustaceous rock on the seabed reaching ever up to the underbelly of the boat. He released the main halliard from its staghorn cleat, allowing the sail to drop. Michaelis started the engine so that they could manoeuvre alongside the wooden jetty.

"*Eh re koumbare,* mind your step there!" shouted Andreas over the noise of the fifty-horsepower engine. "Don't fall in, in your hurry to meet this woman. She must be *ligo* special"

"Oh she's just a good friend." As he leapt ashore John recognized an element of personal doubt that had crept into his reply. "Be back in just under an hour. If she has come at all, she should have cleared the plane and baggage checks by then."

"We'll be here waiting. You'll probably find us propping up Theo's bar over by the jetty. Here are the keys to the car. Catch!"

He waited whilst every passenger went through passport formalities and then customs. A certain annoyance with himself crept in for having built up his hopes too far. Yes, he had argued with himself, she might not come but ninety five percent of his brain had been convinced she would in fact be there. He checked with the desk in the small airport that all the passengers had disembarked and gone through. She hadn't arrived. His disappointment showed visibly on his downcast face.

He turned to go out of the door, all his plans in ruins. In the car on the way to the airport he had imagined all the males on the desks raising their heads and following her long legs through the checking line, making comments to themselves and whistling in the air in the Mediterranean fashion. She had always, in the time he had known her, had the ability to turn heads. He painted more mental pictures of the honey blond hair hung loose and very long, the aquiline nose lending her a kind of noble bearing, the ice blue eyes which might have appeared cold to many an observer but to him meaning fresh baltic promise, like the invitation to dive naked into cool Scandinavian lakes in the heat of summer.

Then someone was calling:

"Iannis!"

Although he knew there were a hundred *Iannis'* in that airport alone, the tone and the accent were almost too familiar. He turned to see Undiga, a real live Undiga, coming across the hall from where the telephone booths were situated. As she walked towards him, he noticed her languid gait. It hinted of the confident poise of a woman who had perhaps been trained professionally for ballet or who had maybe spent many years modelling on the top catwalks. Yet, he knew her training had been in the academic field. She had always seemed to him to unite the 'city deb' look with the air of the well-read woman. John Sampson's nagging thoughts returned. She was here but it was possible she had come to finish it all off. Now she had her career, what would such a stunner see in him. An object of mild pity perhaps, a distant memory—an extended holiday romance?

He tried to read her face. She bore the hint of a furrow on her brow, possibly the result of a touch of travel fatigue. He found himself wanting to interpret this as concern on her part to find him, to be with him. Yet another voice suggested that the slight frown might be a precursor to the bad news she would have to announce.

As she came nearer, her eyes seemed to be searching him, too, looking for communicative signals. He tried to ease a welcoming smile to his lips. As they embraced, he knew he should have felt comforted, should have relaxed and then kissed her in a way that would have told her of his need for her but he found himself a little shy. After all he was a little surprised, after initially thinking she had not arrived, and then he was a forty year old man and the place was quite public. Looking past her shoulder, he imagined the whole range of airport attendants in the hall grinning at him and prevented himself from going further. He took her face in his hands and intimated, with the slightest movement of his head, that they should move on outside. He always got that feeling, when he was with her, that he had a part in a movie with the hottest screen goddess of the day. He felt a whole world looking on, channeling their fantasies through what he and Undiga might enact. But the fear that it couldn't last for ever still gripped him, that somehow the scriptwriter would have him written out and he would suddenly no longer be in the picture.

They each picked up a bag in one hand and, arms around each other's waist, made their way out to the car. Once seated, he leaned over to kiss her gently for he did not want to seem to be sending cold messages out to her.

"Undiga you look beautiful! Welcome back to Cyprus!"

"Hmmm are you sure I'm welcome?' she asked with just a hint of a quizzical smile. "You didn't seem too warm in there"

Damn, he thought, just the impression I didn't want to put over.

"Undiga. I've been waiting for this . . . ."

He stopped in case he should give too much away or open himself to more wounding when the crunch came.

"Don't worry. I know when I am not wanted," she continued lightly.

He knew she was playing with him, like a cat might with a ball of wool, but all the same he was concerned that this might be just the lead up to an ending.

"Don't say things like that, will you Undiga!"

God, he thought, I'm messing up here. I'm really messing this up!

"What happened to you, anyway? You didn't come through on the Bergen flight. I waited for every single passenger to go through"

"Ah they put an extra flight on today. I was on the second one! I've been here for an hour trying to call that number you once gave me"

As he put the car into gear and moved off toward the harbour, he recalled that he had given her the International School number when she had last been here four months ago. She wouldn't have got much joy from there. The school had shut for the summer holidays in early June. He had never had a telephone in Tremithousa. He lived in the style of the simple villager. If people wished to contact him, they came along in person or they wrote letters.

"Well, believe me, Undiga I'm over the moon that you are here. I've got a surprise in store for you today"

"Hmm I wonder what that could be."

"Hope you don't get sea sick or anything like that! We are going to take a little boat journey"

"Sounds different! Where are we off to? Egypt?"

"A little nearer than that. Let it be a surprise!"

His plans had been set. He hoped they would not go wrong.

A little later, John was releasing the mooring ropes from the bollards on the jetty, waving to Andreas and Michaelis who were not going with them, not on such a special day, but who would drive over to Amorosa to meet them at six that evening. The plan was to moor the boat there and Andreas would drive them back to John's house in Tremithousa.

He put the engine into reverse. When he had reached the two fathoms mark, he changed into forward throttle and swept the bow of *Priest Apollo* round to face out to sea. He and Undiga's relationship had belonged to this coast ever since their first encounter in the taverna at Tremithousa. The craggy township of Paleopaphos, built into and along the shallow cliffs, was to their right. It was there where the pilgrims of old, arriving from all parts of the ancient Hellenic world, would have disembarked before joining the pilgrimages to Aphrodite's temples at Paphos and at Kouklia. Being at sea, looking backing at the coastline, gave John the feel of seeing through the pilgrim's eye when, after a long journey, the traveler would first catch sight of his goal. He knew that, if they had approached from the Phoenician coast, where now Lebanon and its neighbours lay, they might well have taken the shortest crossing to Cyprus which would have taken them somewhere near present day Limassol. Then they would have followed the coast westward to Paphos passing first the wonderful fifth Century BC town and amphitheatre established at Kourion, and then, an hour's sail or so on, looking high to the right to see the imposing temple to the Goddess at Kouklia.

The anometer showed a south-westerly of fifteen knots, a gentle breeze but enough to merit putting up the sails. John handled the ropes while Undiga changed into her bikini bottom. The foresail untwirled from the fore stay where it had been tied. Then the sheets were pulled tight so the sails could steadily fill with wind.

"This is the life, John! Ah it's a different world from that lawyer's office in Oslo, I can tell you."

Undiga stretched out along the foredeck of the 38 footer. She had oiled her arms and legs with factor 24. Her pale skin needed protection from the hot southern rays. Despite being aware of this, she kept her breasts bare, as always when she sunbathed. The tilt of her long nipples, aimed up at the cloudless sky, had John gazing at them and desiring her. When he got the boat out a little further, he could engage the self-steering gear and go up front to sit with her. He would still need to watch out for other approaching sea craft but he could give way to his desire to hold her close.

Paphos harbour lay on their path to the West, its Lusignan fort, built on the ruins of an earlier Byzantine castle, signaling entrance to what, from the twelfth to the sixteenth centuries, would have been a strategic port in the Christian battle with the expanding Ottomans. John knew that, if he turned North west and sailed to the Greek island of Castellorizo and on to Kos and Rhodes, he would find very similar fortifications in their main harbours, silent monuments, as were the present day British barracks in Cyprus, to the geopolitical importance of that area throughout the last two millenia. But Paphos carried a more personal,more emotional, message for himself and Undiga. It was from Paphos that it had all developed, when they had met in the harbour and planned their motorbike trips to Drepanum and other places in the Akamas peninsula.

They would now sail round the south western coast, weaving their way past the jutting headlands that sprang out from that very same Akamas peninsula; past Coral Bay and on to Lara where the sea turtles favoured the beaches for laying their eggs. They would pass Drepanum and coast round towards Latchi near where *Fontana Amorosa* lay. The name, John knew, was Italian for 'fountain of love' and it was another reminder—as if one needed another, he thought—of the connections the island had to the Goddess of fertility. He read the paragraph written about it in the Mediterranean Pilot book that lay open before him:

'Although the fountain itself is disappointing, a sort of muddy artesian well, there is a beautiful lagoon around the small reef that walls off the central approach to the wooded bay of Amorosa, where the swimming is famed to be extraordinary. Mycenean, Doric and Roman archaeological remains lie half submerged in the bay like a forgotten atlantis—the result of shattering earthquakes that hit the island in the first century AD.'

By the time they could see the sea caves of Drepanum looming white to starboard, the steering had been locked on to a course for three quarters of an hour and Sampson and Undiga had been cradling each others heads, kissing sometimes gently, sometimes passionately, as they re-accustomed themselves to each other's caress. John's confidence that he was still in with a chance was returning, as she responded so naturally to his touch.

"Remember that place, Undiga? Drepanum?"

"How could I ever forget it, John. It was there we first really discovered each other and there that we were nearly drowned by the freak waves."

He looked back confidently at her and kissed her lightly on her nose.

"You learned to climb that day. Look on the bright side of things."

"Yes and, as you can see from my letters, I've been doing weekend climbing, ever since."

"What letters?" joked John. "I only ever received one"

"But I did call you several times and I sent postcards! I'm sorry John. I'm notoriously poor at letter writing and you don't use computer for the email, but that doesn't mean to say I haven't been thinking of you. I had telepathic communication with you! Didn't you feel it?"

"All right I'll let you off this time. Tell me if you are getting a telepathic message now though."

He kissed her full on to the lips, his tongue searching for hers. He felt the impulses shoot through his body and hers. He wanted to savour it all, however; stretch the experience out as long as he could. He pulled away and they sat up a little, propping their backs against the base support of the mast.

"You haven't told me how the TV programme went yet, John. It all went off OK?"

"Yes, well. The producer liked the outcome and I just got a message at the Poste Restante this morning from Margo, the production assistant, saying that the executive editors are really pleased that I made the episode so personal. I think I told you in the letter—yes the one I wrote two weeks ago—how I had, on the spur of the moment, changed all my notes and linked the mythology of Aphrodite with the survival of the flowers. The moment kind of just came alive, so much so I included parts of my own story, too."

"You didn't include me though, did you?"

"No, I didn't want to make it *that* personal"

"Oh, I am disappointed! I want to be in your documentary!" As she said this, she pursed her lips in the manner of the spoilt little girl.

He reached over again, close to her face, and looked into the flickering pools of blue. "You should have been, I suppose, but I didn't want to put you in competition with the mistress of the island. She has her ways of getting what she wants you know."

Nowadays he could lightly joke about these things. He no longer wanted to think of any other goddess or to invest her with powers. He needed some answers from the real live one in front of him.

"Undiga you are very beautiful. There must be a host of men who would love just to walk by your side—why me ? What can I offer you?"

"John, some men do say I am beautiful and I get a lot of attention, more than I really want. But, as soon as I open my mouth and utter what I think is an intelligent sentence, they back off. You know, I've come to the conclusion that men are terrified of women who have any brain. I think that image of the dumb blonde is conjectured by men to suit the average male's taste for a pretty partner who won't challenge his dominance. So you were refreshingly unafraid of me and you challenged my brain, as well as my hormones. Get the picture?"

Sampson felt quite honoured that she had singled him out in this way but he was wary. His first wife had been an intelligent woman. Intelligent women could also have ways of wrapping men round their little fingers. Now in her late twenties, Undiga might just be responding to some pretty demanding hormones which were telling her to settle down and build a nest. He had come along at the right time—handy so to speak. Was he prepared to rush into another domestic scenario so soon after the other had collapsed? The thought brought on a moment of unexpected panic. He laid Undiga's head slowly back onto the towel that stretched over the fore-deck then retreated to the wheel. He disengaged it from automatic and turned the boat straight for the high cliffs of Akamas.

He could see the wooded bay of Fontana in the distance and a couple of vehicles winding their way around the high track that ran along the cliff tops above the bay. He approached carefully, for there were spurs of reef here and there that would make short work of the bottom of any boat. As he approached where the water tumbled lightly over the main coral wall that guarded the mouth of the bay, he let all sails drop and prepared to reverse engines slightly so that he could halt the forward thrust of the boat. Practising all the theory he had read in the 'Day Skipper Manual,' he stopped the boat at a safe twenty yards from the reef. As he lowered anchor, he waited for the rope to stop unwinding, indicating that the anchor had lodged on the bottom. When he saw the rope cease its downward roll, he reversed slowly so that he could pay out the chain on the seabed. Four yards into reverse he stopped the boat to adjust the catenary of the anchor rope. He quietened the engine and looked at his watch. It was 11-45 am.

They would eat, if all went according to plan, around one o'clock. But first he would have to catch their lunch.

"Undiga, fancy a swim?"

"Looks fabulously clear water. Yes I'm in there"

"Can you see where the water changes colour, about twenty yards over there on the other side of the reef?"

She strained her vision through the bright haze of the summer day:

"Yes I think I can." It's like—here its crystal blue and there it goes kind of eau de nile—green as pea soup"

"Well, it is definitely not soupy when you're swimming in it. It is deep, clear and exciting, with fish everywhere feeding off the circular reef. That's where we'll find our lunch, inside the lagoon."

He leaned down and extracted the speargun from its box. He normally didn't fish with such an instrument. Back in England, on the Thames or on the Kennet canal, it had been fly fishing. Not that one method was preferable to another. He often thought fishing with a line was as bad as, if not worse than, spearing them. The fish's death was slower when caught on the hook or for that matter by a net. Anyway, today he needed a quick solution for lunch so the gun would have to do.

"Put those on, Undiga," he said, throwing some protective rubber shoes to her and a mask and snorkel.

"What are we going to be able to see, John?" she asked as she expanded the shoes over her feet.

"Oh just about everything you might possibly think could exist in the sea, plus parts of the ancient city state of Soloi, now submerged. All I have to do is put a mermaid in it and we have fantasia under the sea," he laughed.

They splashed into the clear blue, jumping off the 'Priest Apollo's' leeside and surfacing to pull their snorkeling masks down over their faces. Having swum the short distance over to the reef wall, John took Undiga by the hand and showed her the way to scramble upright over the outer reef wall, their heads now well above the surface of the water.

"Steady here! That reef can cut you badly. That's it. Let go of my hand now and paddle with your hands to steady yourself. A couple of steps more and we just fall over the edge of the wall. One . . . two . . . . Over we go!"

Undiga and John found themselves buoyed up on the surface of the lagoon, peering down into a bowl of extravagant colour, with myriads of fish competing for the tasty morsels that the reef provided. The smaller fish could easily enter the lagoon, through holes in the walls of the reef, but larger fish that preyed on them were largely excluded. John could see what he was looking for, however; a medium sized swordfish, perhaps a metre and a half in length, swirling in the depths waiting for its opportunity to seize the *gavra,* its favourite food. At present these tiny fish seemed consummately distracted, sucking at small sections of coral. The bulk of the swordfish was in its length, although it was a meaty fish. This one would have been able to have pushed his way through a smallish aperture, motivated as it would have been by the prospect of a craze of a feed on the reef. Little did it suspect that it was now the hunted, for John, having indicated to Undiga what he was after, quickly took his chance.

Blowing up through the snorkel to clear the tube, he submerged himself, diving at a ninety degree angle to the surface, the safety catch pulled back on the deadly spear apparatus.

The long fish swept its body up to engulf the swarm of *gavra* as it rose, straining its white belly. The sunlight flashed upon its gills and side scales creating a kaleidoscopic lightshow, as it swirled to disorientate its packed prey. Sampson caught another flash of pure white and released the shot. The first spear missed, hit the reef wall and sent a cloud of dust out into the lagoon. The swordfish knew now it was challenged and dashed to escape to the far wall. John's second dart found its mark, however, piercing the side of the fish. It immediately pulled away to bottom trailing the wire attached to the spear now lodged within it. John let the wire roll out as he needed to get back up for air. He ascended quickly and gasped out for air on the surface.

Establishing his footing on a ledge of the wall, he pushed the mask up on his head, secured his back and pressed the automatic reel-in device. The whine it produced told him the wire was coming back in. The weight he felt on the end also indicated that the catch was struggling at the end of that wire.

Undiga was watching the entire operation from her vantage position, lying prone on the surface of the lagoon. She could see the fish rising, fighting, trying to pull back down to the security of the depths. At that moment she was overcome with pity for the fish, desperately trying to hold on to its life. She wished she could somehow free it but the whole process seemed inexorable. She lay there on the surface, reflecting on the lesson on symbiosis that the coral reef provided. Every living creature survived on other living organisms and, she supposed, John and herself were somewhere on that food chain; at the top of it to be precise. Still she was aware of an abhorrence that John could be the prime perpetrator of this killing. Blood started to seep from the side of the fish. She had to look away. This was not the John that she had known. He had been the victim then and she had loved his nature, sturdy in his opinions but sensitive to the environment in all its forms. Was he changing? Had he already changed so much?

The fish was out, its long snout stabbing the air. John carefully laid it on the rocky shelf; then he used the butt end of gun to stun the fish and then, with a second blow to its head, put it out of its agony. Securing the fish in a crevice with the harpoon, he replaced his mask and returned to Undiga. He gave her the thumbs up sign. She had brought her head out of the water and had witnessed that the fish no longer struggled. She looked closely at John. He actually appeared to be enjoying this business. There was an element, it appeared to her, of the aggressive in him today.

Sampson indicated he would lead her over to the far perimeter of the circular basin of the lagoon. They joined hands as they floated and kicked their way across. Undiga noticed that the walls changed in shape and what looked like arches of coral appeared deep below them. Then pillars came into view, some lying on their sides, others appearing to prop each other up. Large plinths, one with carved writings on, crumbled under and over the sharded pieces of what would once have been drinking cups and water jars. Fish of all varieties swam inquisitively amongst the ruins, as though trying to establish what such an obviously man-made structure should be doing here in their water zones. Undiga took up her throwaway underwater camera which hung attached by a small chain to a bracelet on her wrist and clicked away, as she moved over the remains of ancient Soloi.

John saw her swim ahead of him, her breasts splayed sideways by the draught of the water, her hair trailing behind, her sensuous bottom following the rhythm of her leg kicks. He moved rapidly forward, diving shallowly underneath her, turning on his back and gazing up at her face which was slightly stretched, the eyes intent inside the mask. He reached up to touch her breasts then to trace his fingers down the contours of her sides. As John came up for air, she changed her position. Treading water, she had pulled off her mask and now he could see her expression, a little surprised, a little beckoning and just a hint of fearfulness. Taking her by one arm, he swam her over to the wall where they were able to get some kind of footing. He caught a large outcrop of coral in one hand and took her by the waist with the other pulling her in to his eager body.

For Undiga John was a changed man. His transformation was a little frightening and unexpected. The ease with which he had killed the fish, the strong way he handled the boat and yet the unease with which he had handled her, upon their meeting at the airport made her wonder whether it was the same man she had fallen in love with seven months before. On top of all this, here she was being pulled toward him in a lagoon in Cyprus, when only this morning she had been in rainy Oslo. She felt momentarily disorientated. Many different feelings swept by her in the split second before she felt John's urgency and the muscled legs wrapping round her. She realized that she was also strangely excited, wanting to give in entirely to the masterly ways of the man who, at this moment, was holding her in embrace and was kissing her passionately, more passionately than she had ever been kissed before.

She surrendered to the moment and delicious sensations filled mind and body as John and herself explored every contour of each other's bodies until, the lower parts of their bodies floating upward, they locked themselves together, feet flapping excitedly on the surface of the water

Lunch was considerably later than he had planned it. The fish smelt extraordinarily good to John who was squeezing more lemon on to it, as he fried it on the gaz burner. He had also set up the smaller gaz cooker to take a little rice. In the ice box on the deck were two bottles of Champagne, not the cheap but friendly Duc De Nicosie, the local produce, but Dom Perignon, given to him as a leaving present by the International School when the school year had finished in June. The food was now nearly ready. Undiga was showering in the cabin. After their closeness in the lagoon, John's remaining fears had been totally allayed.

The bay lay empty except for a pleasure boat moored up inside the coral wall near the shore, where a group of people were barbecuing. John knew this was the twice-daily pleasure boat from Latchi. The captains knew the sole narrow pathway through the coral reef and their tourists could see the full ruins of the submerged agora of Soloi through the glass bottoms of the boats, as they led them to the shoreline. One of the day trippers must have brought his sailboard with him for a single windsurfer could be seen at the other end of the bay near the shore, circling two small empty fishing boats.

Undiga arrived on deck with a white cotton wrap-round that accentuated her curvaceous form. She kissed John lightly on the nose and, sitting opposite him on the fold-up chair, reached down for the champagne bottle. In the action of bending to the side, John saw her motion suddenly arrested and her eyes locked on to something in the distance.

"John look over there. That windsurfer. Is he alright? He seems to be struggling"

John looked behind him in the direction of the shore. Only a minute ago he had seen the surfer circling the fishing boats. Now he could see that he was in the shallow water and standing up waving his arms. He could hear him shouting, too, since the curved shape of the high cliffs above ricocheted sound out beyond the confines of the bay. It was an English voice and all John could hear were long screeching and terrified cries of 'Help! Help me!'

The first thing that entered John's mind was a shark. Sharks, mostly unagressive but large enough to bite, were beginning to infest the Mediterranean as the sea turned ever saltier. The reefs here in this bay would prove attractive to them too. The man must have fallen off the windsurfer and attracted a shark. John could see too that the party of people on the shore at the other end of the bay were oblivious to his plight. They were playing music and some were dancing. None appeared to be looking in the direction of the stricken boardsailer.

He quickly turned off both gaz burners.

"The champagne will have to stay on ice Undiga. We'll take the shore dinghy through the reef to go see what's up. It will skim through without a problem. Grab that green first aid box from the drawer under the helm."

For the second time that day he took the spear gun from its box and chose two heavy barbed spears. He might need something strong for this job. Then he quickly let down the dinghy boat, put Undiga on the ladder by which she descended into the small rubber boat and followed her. Three minutes after they had first spotted the surfer's predicament, they were on their way, Jon quickly paddling the boat through a small break in the reef. The windsurfer continued to scream and, as they approached, they could see that he stood transfixed in the water looking up. It seemed that in his terror he did not dare look down.

John came in close to him and shouted:

"What's the matter friend—what has got hold of you?"

"I don't know! Its my leg. All of my right leg. I can't move"

Then John realized it would not have been a shark. Their attacks were sudden and frenzied. This man seemed to be held fast by something. A stonefish! That's what it is, thought Sampson. In his readings on marine biology he had read of the lethal injection delivered by the deadly stonefish, sea cousin of the scorpion but much more venomous. If you stood on one of these creatures it immediately opened its spine and injected you with a poison that could kill within twenty minutes.

Now Sampson felt the dire urgency of the situation. The young man of about twenty years was whimpering in panic, his legs rooted to the spot but his arms thrashing wildly

"Undiga, you start waving and shouting at those people on the shore. You have got to draw their attention. I'll just swim in closer to the man's leg. Don't worry! I think I know what it is"

Then with a word of comfort to the struggling young man telling him to relax, assuring him that everything would now be fine, he dived into the shallow sea water and, eyes open in the stinging salty water, sought out the offender.

It did not take him long to discover the reason for the sail boarder's apparent paralysis. It had nothing to do with his first two assumptions. A huge anchor prong had entered the base of the man's foot and its barbed catch was jutting out at the top of his shin, just under the knee. Sampson followed the chain and then the rope up to the small blue and white fishing vessel that bobbed on the surface of the water, over to his left. It took only seconds to work out that, as he had fallen from his board, he had jumped back and, shallow as the water was, had landed directly on the iron protusion of an anchor that was five times the size required for a small fishing boat. The monstrosity must have been taken off an old tugboat or similar vessel.

He surfaced and found himself able to stand easily beside the stricken Englishman. The first thing was to put him at his ease or he feared he might collapse with fright and panic.

"I know you are wondering what has gotten hold of you friend. It is nothing serious. Please relax. Nothing that can really harm you"

"I can't see from here and I can't lift my leg" the young man moaned. "What in hell is it?"

"You've stood on an anchor. It is a great heavy thing and it must feel like a ton weight is pulling you down. But believe me it is not going to kill you. We'll cut you free in a minute."

Sampson could see that Undiga had atttracted the attention of two men in the beach party who were making their way along the beach toward them.

"Well done Undiga. Now row the dinghy right up to us here."

She followed his directions and soon the young man was able to hold the side of the rubber boat. Sampson was wondering, however, how he was going to free the victim's leg and then how they could get leg and anchor, for he could see they were both firmly attached, to hospital in Paphos, twenty five kilomteres round the coast. The first thing he needed was a knife to cut the retaining rope from its anchor chain.

The two men from the beach party, one obviously swarthy and Cypriot, the other a sunburned tourist, had arrived on the shore about fifteen metres away. Sampson shouted over to them explaining what had happened and asked one of them to run back to fetch a sharp knife. Neither could really believe what had happened so, ignoring his instructions, they both came paddling in to see. When they saw the size of the anchor embedded up the whole course of the lower leg from foot to knee they let out soft whistles of amazement.

"Holy Jeesus," said the sunburned tourist in what was clearly a Dublin accent. "Isn't this somethin'!"

"*Doxa tou Theou!*" whispered the Cypriot under his breath. "What can we do about this?"

"I need something sharp" replied Sampson. "Have you got a knife . . . ."

Before he finished the sentence, he remembered the sharp barbs of the big spears he had taken along with the gun.

"Undiga hand me down one of the spears attached to the side of the gun. Just unclip the little retainer hinge. You my friend"—here he was addressing the Cypriot—"support the lad under his armpits, he must be feeling exhausted by now. And you"—now he looked at the Irishman—"go see if there is a mobile phone anywhere and call emergency services out. The fire brigade as well! They have cutting equipment!"

"I know someone has a phone on the beach. The captain I think. He was using it only ten minutes ago" said the Irishman, turning hurriedly toward the beach.

"Please hurry!" Sampson added as took the long jagged end of the projectile in one hand and, finding the line of rope in the other, traced it till it met the anchor chain. He then retraced the rope back a foot or two, held his spear like a knife and began to slice through the rope. Because it was wet, the thick strands of hemp resisted the cut and it took him two or three sawing attempts to get through each strand. Determinedly he kept at it till eventually it broke apart and he was able to lift part of the chain with the remaining short end of the rope.

Now for the tough bit, thought John. We'll never lift him into the dinghy with that weight piercing his leg. The pain will kill him.

He turned to the Cypriot who was still busy supporting the hapless windsurfer under both his arms.

"Ok now we'll take him out onto the beach. You take the left arm and leg and I'll take the right ones. We'll lift him very very gently, anchor attached and all, and float him out!"

Sampson took the right arm of the young man and placed it round his neck, attempting at the same time to lift the leg and support the anchor which pulled at the tendons. As the leg came up, the young man's white face screwed up in intense pain. He let out a frightening scream then promptly fainted. John tried to support the anchor better and rushed the semi conscious patient the fifteen yards to shore. On the pebbles the Cypriot and he laid down their human load, the massively swollen leg limb lying in the edge of the sea for coolness and bouyancy. John attempted to bring the young Englishman round, lightly slapping his cheeks and attempting to talk him back to full consciousness.

Undiga had paddled in to the shore and lodged the dinghy up on the pebbles. She stared unbelievingly at the leg, one large black iron prong gaping up through the hole it had punctured, the other barb and the handle still attached to its chain trailing off the foot, its awkward shape and size necessitating that the foot lie on its side on the shale of the beach. Incredibly, she thought, there was no blood anywhere only a whiteness in the swelling as though all blood had been squeezed elsewhere into the body.

A crowd gathered round, as the picnicking tourists arrived from their barbeque spot. All looked on in amazement and in shock. The young man had just come round again and, having once more realized his predicament, had started to moan. A girl who appeared to know him well was supporting his neck. Undiga could hear the very articulate captain of the pleasure cruiser who had just come off his mobile, telling John that Paphos police had requested assistance from the British Royal Air Force based at Akrotiri.

"Yes they've already scrambled a rescue team it seems. Take them only fifteen minutes or so to fly round the coast. The Paphos ambulance service would take hours to get here and then there is no passable road down to the bay. We would have to carry our friend here up the hillside to the high road above us. In his present state that would be impossible . . . . *adyneeto, neh re* . . . totally impossible!"

107

Undiga felt relieved that help was on its way but it would take a long time for the shock to pass. She was still stunned by it all. Here she had been back in Cyprus for only four and a half hours and so much had taken place. She had lived in America for four years and, although dramatic things happened, they had never happened to her! After meeting John, tension and drama seemed to her to have been the order of the day. But, all the same, she remembered herself being the cool logical part of the relationship. In Oslo, she reflected, you read about things happening but nothing, in four months there, had ever happened to make her feel involved in any drama. Today's events were a rude new reawakening to the untamed Cyprus. Goddesses and monsters, the mythological and the real, the land and the sea, danger and love threw themselves up in front of you like a series of swirling cinematographic images. She felt dizzy with the impact of this, her first day back. She lay back on the beach and tried to close her eyes.

Her head was still swimming with pictures as she saw the helicopter swoop down to land on the beach. The team of medics soon had the young Englishman, still attached to his personal anchor and chain, on to a stretcher and into the Sea King helicopter. The picnickers were making their way back to their rallying point and herself and John were rowing out to the *Priest Apollo*.

After securing the dinghy, John had turned his attentions back to the gaz cooker.

"Let's get tucked into that fish and the Champagne shall we?" declared John.

"Not for me John, thank you. I think I need to just lie down for a while in the shade"

John reheated the fish and sipped the champagne. Undiga watched him from her cool spot under the awning and mused at the changes in her man, till eventually she fell into a deep sleep. The heat and excitement had drawn on a very deep sleep indeed.

She did not clearly remember anything she had dreamt about, as she found herself heading through Kathikas, in Andreas' car, on the back roads up to Peyia and Tremithousa. It was night and a cool breeze fluttered through the window. All she could remember was John waking her and leading her off the boat at Latchi fishing port, where Andreas had been waiting for them in the car. Then she must have fallen back to sleep again. She was aware of John's arm around her and of the strength that seemed to radiate out of him.

In her mind was a long string of images that was a reminder of her day. Exotically coloured fish darted amongst ruins and anchors. Several semblances of John came to her, one hard faced with speargun in hand, another strong, lifting the windsurfer out of the water, and yet another of him kissing her, possessing her in the lagoon. Superimposed on the snapshots, as on a picture collage, was a statue of Aphrodite she had seen in the in-flight magazine that morning. In her present sleepy condition, she did not want to make too much sense of the day or of the series of pictures that flashed across her mind. She wanted only for the car to stop in Tremithousa and, there, to sleep a deep untroubled sleep.

She was aware, however, that tomorrow—yes, tomorrow when she could think straight—she would have to begin to come to terms with the new persona that John had taken on and to assess exactly what had happened to her self, in the course of her first day back in Cyprus.

John's thoughts were not so puzzled or confused. He felt confident that the girl beside him was still his. He determined that, for the duration of Undiga's month of vacation, he would cast all doubts about the future of their relationship to the wind.

EPISODE 11

Tremithousa honey

Waking in the village to shafts of sunlight, sloping through the open door and windows, was one of the pleasures Undiga had become used to, during the four weeks of her summer holiday back on the island. The sounds of rural Cyprus filled the air. Cockerels called out stridently over the background chirping of the sparrows and vineyard birds, the donkeys in the meadows behind the main street braying to greet the day. It was a summer morning in Tremithousa.

It is little wonder, she mused, as she set her eye upon the jasmine that the slight breeze had pushed through the open side window, that so many people from Northern Europe wanted to spend time here. The weather, although it could be very humid now in early July, was temperate ninety per cent of the year and, at certain times like these summer early mornings, gentle but warm breezes could woo a person, used to only inhospitable northern cold, into a love affair with the island.

A sense of contentment filled Undiga as she slowly came round from sleep on this the morning before her departure back to Norway. She had never enjoyed such pure relaxation as that she had experienced, following the raw excitement of the first day of her arrival on the island for her month's break with John. They had sampled the *mezes* in other remote villages, watched the Cypriot folk dances, and gone sailing. Many days she had simply whiled away hours on remote beaches while John had gone off exploring for specimens. She had watched him play Camillo in 'The Winter's Tale' at Kourion, where she had sat sipping champagne on the stone steps of the ancient Greek theatre with the McKenzies and the George family, as the actors of the Anglo-Cypriot Theatre group tried to make their voices carry above the wash of the sea that lay behind and below the stage. Then there had been walks through deep pinewoods on the upper slopes of Mt Olympos, picnics in the clearings at Stavros Tis Stokkas and all over the Akamas, a day's excursion across the green line to see the Karpassian mountains. It had all been one continuous treat for her.

She stirred in the bed reaching for John, only to suddenly remember that he had got up an hour earlier, saying he had important things to do. But she could hear his voice. He was talking to the village priest and the honey seller in the kitchen, negotiating the price of a bucket of honey. John was using very fluent Greek now, she noted, even adding all the *cha* sounds that marked Cypriot dialect from mainland Greek. She herself had learned enough Greek to get by and recognised John's flattering comment to Demetri :

"Eese chakkos, koumbare mou Demetri".

John must have got the price he wanted, for him to refer to Demetri in such glowing terms as 'my fine mate.' She had got to know most of the characters in the village, having encountered them down at Soulla's taverna. Demetri, she remembered, had a reputation for striking a very hard bargain.

She decided it was time to get up. She only had one more day left and John, too, was due to leave Cyprus in ten days time. Better for both of them to use their remaining time to advantage. As Undiga was showering, much laughter emerged from the back door where she could hear the three men, who had moved out to the rear patio, discussing the fruit trees that grew in abundance in long rows stretching the length of the strema and a half of land which made up the back garden. They were talking of ripe young lemons and what they reminded them of. Undiga chuckled to herself as she thought of the Cypriot down-to-earth sense of humour, whereby even the granmas and the priests would laugh at what, by western standards, might seem very risque. As she let the cool water resurrect her still-sleep-bound limbs she quickly ran through the coming day's programme. Tennis first. She would partner John against a couple of English people they had met recently at the taverna. The game was to be in Kamares, an up-market holiday village ten kilometres further up into the mountains, where most of the British ex-patriate community had their homes and where there was an English-run club where John and herself were to have lunch afterwards.

The afternoon would include shopping for some of the Paphos village craft produce, such as woven baskets and delicate lace work, presents for her family back in Norway. A quick siesta and then the evening was to be spent having dinner at their favourite spot—the taverna here in Tremithousa. Then an early night because she had an early flight in the morning and, more important, she wanted intimate time with John.

She knew now that all her reservations about continuing the relationship had disappeared. Her nagging doubts about the changes in him had been quietened after that long hot day, her first back in Cyprus a month ago. She had opened herself up to him telling him of how she had felt when he had cut short her kiss at the airport and when he had stood with that harpooned fish dripping blood onto his hands. She had come to realize that John was aware, in a strange way, of his own metamorphosis but that he didn't feel he had fundamentally changed. He had argued his case about the fish and told her of his own fears; that she might not have arrived from Norway and about a straightforward shyness of displaying too much affection in public.

She had then blamed herself for not writing to him from Norway, for not being sensitive enough to his needs. But, fundamentally, she had felt thoroughly relieved that their relationship could go on. The more she had reflected on his new-found confidence on the boat and the way he had taken charge of the situation with the stricken sailboarder, the more convinced she became that this could only be positive. Now he was no longer a victim, though that special time of their relationship, their beginning, had been precious to her. Now he was so ready to take the lead, to use his knowledge of the island, like a key, she imagined, unlocking the series of doors that gave clues to the mystery that was Cyprus.

She knew now that she loved him.

The echoing thump of the tennis balls going to and fro on the middle court of Kamares Club had fallen silent. The two couples were making their way back to the club. David Eames, who with his wife had been on the opposite side of the court, was asking, in the high pitched declamatory tones of the ex-British officer :

"So, John, now you are part of the community, so to speak,—you know lived here for a bit—got to know the place—how about getting yourself a bit of a pad up here in Kamares and settling down in the Med eh?"

He'd heard it before. The temptation on the mountain top. And indeed it was at great height, for the Kamares club, whose swimming pool they were now skimming on their way into the bar, had been cut out of the bowl of mountain that supplied views for thirty kilometres down to Peyia and from there to Coral bay and beyond. The vista was spectacular but as John surveyed the club and its surrounding villas, thirty or forty of which made up the centre of Kamares, he knew that this would never be a place he could live.

"There are three considerations that come to mind, David. First this is no longer Cyprus—this is a British enclave run to British tastes and British rules. Now I don't want to upset anybody's perceptions but Cyprus is first of all for the Cypriots, it seems to me, reflecting their culture and their way of life."

John could see that he had already made David recoil. The latter hadn't expected, it was clear to see, that a fellow Englishman would begin to challenge the comfortable existence that Kamares provided for those expats who had become accustomed to enjoying the all-year-round sunshine and ease of life that Western Europe could not provide. Sampson was, however, determined to make his point. It wasn't David he needed to attack, he knew, but the whole principle of foreigners not integrating with the already established communities.

"I think we can all enjoy Cyprus in our own way, John" retorted the retired British army colonel in a somewhat peeved tone of voice. "Kamares is a great place to live!"

"Yes, David, I agree. Kamares is a lovely spot but there are no Cypriots living here. In fact it is ninety nine per cent British."

He paused to look at the bar menu.

"And look at this! The menu caters for your steak and two veggers when they come off the golf course. There are no Germans here at all. They are all living in a colony over at Polis, probably munching their way through Pfeffer Schnitzels. There are no Scandinavians here, they are all on the nudist beaches by Ayia Napa. If you see what I mean, apart from the weather, you may as well be living back in England and the other Europeans in their respective countries."

"And Tremithousa. What has that been like?" asked David, beckoning to the waiter in the black trousers and dickie bow, to take a drinks order.

John had been quick to detect the note of condescension in the way David had said 'Tremi-thous-a.' It had a reputation for being a slow village. Nothing ever changed rapidly there. It was the butt of many local jokes.

"Well, first of all I am only temporary there. Even so, I have been a guest in a real village where ninety nine per cent of the population are Cypriot, where the taverna has a flagstone floor and excellent local food, where all the characters of the village, and there are many of them, appear each evening at the bottom of the hill to gather in their respective camps, nationalist or communist, depending on which football team they support and which newspaper they read."

"Yes they're a political lot these Cypriots, aren't they, John? Oh bye the way what are you having—beer?"

"Yes please. A Keo for me and a glass of Aphrodite for Undiga."

David gave his order and came back to his argument.

"John, we always get these purist arguments, normally from artist types and intellectuals like yourself. The truth is that all that claptrap is sentimentalist. Of course we must move with the times. The offshore British community has the money to lead Cyprus into modernization. Just look around you. The standard of housing and of roads and the neat appearance of the club! It's a clean healthy environment."

Sampson waited for his beer to arrive. He was thirsty after the tennis and the July midday heat still permeated the club house, fighting with the air conditioning for control of the temperature. When his *keo* came he took two deep draughts of the lager beer before turning to David again.

"You know, David, you've got a point there. It is clean. But a bit too clinical for me. Then to get it this way you have ripped out trees, bushes, flowers and vegetation. OK so you put a few pots around the place afterwards and bring a few rose bushes over from the mother country and Bob's your uncle—little England—a little clean plastic England."

"In any place in the world we have to uproot some of the countryside to build a place to live. You are very aware of that, John"

Undiga and Anne, David's wife, fidgeted uncomfortably. The gentlemen appeared to be getting into an argument. Undiga knew that it was unlikely that her new man, the 'one year in Cyprus' John Sampson would ever back down on these, his strongest feelings about Cyprus. She suspected that Anne had the measure of her husband too, an ex-Colonel in the British Army, who had completed his commission here on the island. He had been used to living British-style at the Episkopi garrison and he had not been used to being contradicted in his judgments.

"Tell me Undiga, what do Norwegian women tend to drink when they are out? Is there a favourite tipple?"

Undiga knew what Anne was doing and, raising her voice a little and looking over pointedly at John, she said :

"Well, we have this wonderful orange schnappes which is very popular in the winter but we like our lagers, too."

John saw the attempt to change the subject but was having none of it.

"David, what about the language too? This is the only place in the world where Homeric Greek survives. In the mountains here after the passing of millennia, despite hundreds of invasions and occupations, you can still hear words like *Thyra* to depict a door and the peasants still describe their surroundings using the same adjectives that Homer did in the Iliad and the Odyssey. That, and the culture that goes with it, slips away under the pressure of a new British invasion."

"Poppycock! The English language is saving Cyprus from extinction. An English education brings Cypriots into the computer age and allows them to view history with a different perspective. The language that is the lingua franca of the world allows Cypriot businessmen to be at the cutting edge of modern economic investment. Come on, get real John!"

` Despite the attempts of the two women to distract their men with small talk and occasional daggered looks pointed toward their husbands, the two men stuck in to their respective arguments and soon became quite red and heated. Eventually Undiga decided she would break this up. It was her last day in Cyprus and she did not want it spoiled by argument.

"Oh John, don't we have an appointment in Tsada? We are running late already!"

"What appointment in Tsada?"

"You know that quiet lunch we were going to have in Mitsos'place"

She glared at him, to let him realize she was making it up but that he had better quickly start nodding his head or she would not be responsible for her actions.

He caught the import of her look and started to make his rapid departure apologies.

"Ah, well. We'll just have to beg to differ on that one, David. I'm sorry we have to go. I was quite enjoying this little tiff."

"Before you go, John, have a look at this inscription above the bar door. It's one of Solon's axioms. It encourages me to think the ancient Greeks thought much as we English, even if you don't think we really fit in."

John looked up to read the carved Greek lettering.

"*Meethen agan*," he read aloud.

"Sounds good," said Undiga. "But what does it mean and who was this man, Solon?"

It was David Eames who was in first with the answer.

"Means 'Nothing In Excess' my dear and Solon was a sixth century BC Athenian lawmaker who has been credited with laying down the main principles of European law and even philosophy of life. Thing is, old chaps, it's exactly what the British put across when they project their lifestyle abroad. You know 'live and let live' and a healthy sort of compromise—none of these extremist or left wing ideals that always lead to trouble!"

John was walking down the rose-lined pathway that led out to the car park. He looked closely at David Eames and suddenly realized that, had it been a year ago, he might have agreed with him. Oxford was a very reactionary sort of place and many of the sedentary ideas that inhabited the musty rooms of some of the more traditional Dons had rubbed off on him. He knew now that he was changed irrevocably. What was more, he knew it would be hard to change a man like Eames. He knew the spirit of Solon's words flew higher than the barren concept of British compromise, but he didn't want to go into it with him. David Eames would have to have his own personal catharsis, his own meeting with his inner self as he, Sampson, had had, over the last year, before he could start asking the right questions, never mind answering them.

Arriving at the top of the elegant club gardens, he turned back to look down on the sweep of vineyards that rolled down to the sea, dotted here and there with stone huts, the roofs of which were a faded terracotta red. John pointed to the view. He could not resist leaving David Eames with a question.

"Ask yourself, David, honestly and authentically: which belies the motto 'nothing in excess' more, this perfect scene, little changed over the centuries, or this?" He indicated the whitewashed concrete amalgamation of villas and bars that was Kamares. "And whatever you may think of the individual advantages of your village contrasted with the others, does Kamares deserve to use so much of the dam water that comes down from the mountains? So much that the Greek villages below you and on the plain have only a trickle and have regular shortages?"

There was a sting and a blow in these last questions that had David nearly bursting a blood vessel. There had been a lot of bad press recently on this matter and water, John knew, was the most sensitive of issues on Cyprus. If the rains were bad in any given year, the water actually had to be shipped in to the island.

Before David could summon his replies,Undiga and he said a quick goodbye and Undiga even kissed David and his wife on the cheek as a conciliatory token. It was with some feeling of relish, however, that Sampson crawled in behind the wheel of the Volvo Amazon and drove away in the direction of Tsada.

The picnic, on a wall overlooking Tsada, was simple and filling. The two lovers washed down village bread, *lountza* ham and *Kaskavalli* cheese with a bottle of *Domaine d'Achera*. They had cooled their lips with juicy *carpousi*, the large red watermelon with the green skin. Undiga playfully covered John's eyes, in case, as she said, he was contaminated by the view of the golf course, the second stage of which was under development and which was replacing terraced vineyards right under their friend Rosie's house.

Another hour was spent visiting some other villages, picking up basketware and mats and lace which, along with big pots of Tremithousa thyme-honey, Undiga would carry back to her family in Norway. They even found time to pop in to Peggy's café at the crossroads in Upper Paphos.

Noone could really come or go from Paphos without paying their respects to Peggy. She had come out, forty five years before, on a promise, only to suffer a disappointment in love. She had never returned to her native Kerry in Ireland but had run, for forty years now, the main meeting place for Cypriots and expats alike. It served as a bar, an information centre and a functions room. Local gossip was also at a premium.

"I've heard that you are off on your wanderings again John. Just when we thought you and Undiga might settle down here and get yourself legalized, you know by Father Murray!"

"If you mean get married, Peggy, no I don't think we are quite ready for that. And I'm not really wandering. I'm going back to Oxford, or that's the plan, to present a few papers."

117

"It's a wedding we want, not lectures. Nothing like a good wedding! I'll be able to bring out that bottle of Old Bushmills I've been saving. It's been in the cupboard for fifteen years now. I thought that's what they meant when they wrote 'Bushmills 15 years' on the bottle! Ha ha! No, seriously, nobody special ever gets married here!"

Twenty minutes later, as the Volvo Amazon pulled up the hill,. John chuckled to himself. If the bottle of whisky were to wait for Undiga and himself, it would get very dusty indeed. They had discussed all that. Long live their relationship but no tying of any hitches for them, they had agreed.

Seven o'clock had just been tolled out at the small village church back in Tremithousa, as John Sampson and Undiga took their seats in Akis and Soulla's taverna. The noise of the village priest, intoning the orthodox litanies, droned out and along the road that the taverna faced onto. Dusk had just been swallowed into night. The bats swung high in the beams of the awning. John sat very still to really listen to the village and the sounds that had so affected him almost one year ago. Then it had imported unease, something beautiful but alien and therefore somewhat frightening. Now his mind and his emotional self welcomed all the sounds and smells. He felt completely comfortable. The ever present trizonia—the crickets-chirped loudly, the dogs called to each other and to the full round moon. The laughter of the men in the cafeneon opposite drifted over, an earthy laugh of simple people. The red tractor of the Mukhtar was parked up in its usual place. The village headman was on the veranda of the cafeneon and waved over to greet the two foreigners as they took their seats.

No sign of Akis tonight. Soulla, as usual, attended to them quickly putting some cold figs and *staphilia*, the white grapes, on the table as an appetizer. She had just managed the customary "*kali spera, Ianni*", when she rushed off to bring cold bottles of Keo beer. Was it him, John, being a little extra keyed up tonight or did he notice a quickness in Soulla's step, an excitement written on the Cypriot woman's face?

When she returned, she gave Undiga, then John, a big hug and sat down beside them, beaming. Yes, she was bursting to get some news out. He had not seen her smile so broadly since the night Aphrodite, the old donkey, had been brought back to the village into retirement from the wine press.

"Ella" he found himself saying. "Come on, out with it, Soulla! Have you won the *Laiko*?" Remote chance but she might have just won the lottery!

She impressed on them that it was a bit of a story but that in some ways it was better than a lottery win. John and Undiga looked over at each other. What could be such good news?

"*Akis peege sta vouna,*" she ventured.

What! Akis had gone off to the mountains! Had he left Soulla for one of the floozies from the Bonanzo bar?

"*Mou eipe oti ya avton to taverna eteleeose. Ethele na erkete ena gogis. To idio tou patera sou!*"

"What's the *gogis* bit John? I didn't follow," Undiga asked.

"It means a shepherd. Akis has given up the taverna. He has gone off to keep sheep, as his father had done before him."

Soulla's expression changed, with the totally natural actorial posing that Mediterranean folk can display, when storytelling. She took on the look of anger.

"*Ego etypiose polla. Malachos, eepa ego, then eene kreemata ekei apano!*"

"She gave him a good hiding." John could barely hide the smile as he translated. He was thinking of Akis being chased around the taverna. Cypriot women could get very aggressive when annoyed. He imagined the telling off that Akis got—to abandon a profitable business and go off to become a shepherd!

The details came out. Akis had a run down *mantri* left to him by his father and a tiny plot of land to go with it. He didn't feel cut out to be serving all those foreign people. Soulla explained how it had occurred to her that all this was an excuse, so that he could stay out at night, chasing the dancers at the Bonanzo. Then she indicated how she had laid the big frying pan over his head by banging her fist down on the table so hard the grapes jumped off their plate.

"*Ya moto ton ektupesa!*"

Sampson explained with a grin, "She gave him one he wouldn't easily forget"

"Well, is he still up there keeping sheep?" Undiga ventured. "Or did she knock sense into him?"

John translated the question.

Soulla's smile returned

"*Nai, alla kati egene!*"

"Yes, he's up there. But something has happened since. It happened two days ago." He now could not hold back his curiosity.

"What happened? *Ti egene?*"

Soulla lifted her two hands in a dramatic gesture.

"*Evrekete nero!*"

John was amazed.

"You understood Undiga didn't you? Akis . . . Akis has found water!"

"Herre Gud!" said Undiga reverting, in her surprise, to her native Norwegian.

"My God, indeed, Undiga. That's headline news in Cyprus!"

When Soulla had brought out the usual bulgar wheat and yoghurt and delicate *eliopates, the* olive pies in light pastry, and had allowed time for her guests to absorb this dramatic news, she filled them in on how Akis had sunk a bore on the second day back on his father's property. She explained how old Philippos, from the village of *Neo Chorio*, had used the devining stick to lead him to the spot. Four metres down and the water had burst into the air, like an oil strike, at terrific force. First estimates were that there was enough water on that particular mountain table to keep Paphos going for many a year. It was the best news in a century and Akis was the toast of the whole Paphos region. Of course she had forgiven him. Now they had two businesses!

"I'd like to talk to Akis before the Kamares crowd get to him," John whispered over to Undiga. "I'm glad I've got nine days left myself. Maybe I can convince him to route his pipelines well away from Kamares, so that the precious liquid they carry can reach Tremithousa and the plains by Chlorakas and Lemba!"

One hour later a very satisfied couple walked up the hill to the house. They were happy to be together at that moment because the starry Cyprus night and the balmy scent of basil and jasmine, that filled the air, augured well for a night of togetherness. Parting with Undiga tomorrow would be for only a brief while. John would go back to London via Bergen in just over a week.

A certain satisfaction also came from the realization that Paphos had not let them down. Even on Undiga's very last day, she mused, the events that happened around them might have graced the epics that Homer had written and partly centred on the island of Cyprus, where Aphrodite, it seemed, presided over her people. invoking a strange, unspoken and unwritten code of justice.

EPISODE 12

Homage at the altar

The cicadas, called *krikrizonia* in Greek, had been trilling out their discordant tune for the best part of two hours now, but no longer could anyone in Kokkos' bar, on the edge of the village of Ieroskipos, notice the cacophony of their music. The insects lay in the vineyard behind. Sampson fancied they were guiding him in towards his goal just as bees buzzed and danced in the presence of pollen.

It had been warming up inside Kokkos' place, as well as out on the small verandah which bordered the pot-holed road leading directly in from Ieroskipos to Paphos. The bottle of the cheap *Keo cognaki* had replaced a plastic rose as centre piece on the tinnish-blue table and its contents were gradually flushing Sampson's cheeks. Each new glass was accompanied by a new saucerful of *konnes,* for which modern Ieroskipos was famous. To think, he mused, that these monkey-nuts, along with the ubiquitous Turkish Delight, had taken over in a town which had hosted pilgrims from all over the known Greek world 3,000 years before. *Ieroskipos,* as the Guide Book had informed, was the Greek for 'Holy Garden'.

Pilgrims had come in their millions to worship the chief Goddess of Greek culture. They had landed at the ancient port of Paphos—a couple of miles east of the modern one—and processed up to the garden where they would sleep, drugged by the strong night flower scents. Then, in the morning, they had gathered wild flowers and fruit and picked their way up to the altar of Kouklia, presenting them as votive offerings on the great open stone slab. Maidens might have prayed that one day, soon, their beloved young men would return from war or merchant ships to marry them; men would have asked for wives of great beauty and child bearing hips. Mothers might have expressed their longing that their children would settle soon before the great sleep of *Lethe* took them. Middle aged men would have rekindled their sexual fervour, drinking potions mixed by the Temple priestesses who also served as expensive prostitutes.

Tomorrow he would leave Paphos.

Sampson had mixed feelings about that. On the one hand, he told himself, he was on the threshold of a new life. Just exactly what he would do he did not know; did not want to know. There was a new adventure out there. Undiga would be part of it in some way. He would report to his Oxford college, Brasenose, to write up his notes, for he had been booked to give a presentation at the Bodleian Library next month.

"*Re koumbare inda pou skeptese?* Dreaming again?" Kokkos had come in from playing cards up the street. His gravelly voice bespoke long years of cigarettes and *cognaki.*

Sampson was a little upset that his train of thought had been disturbed but then Kokkos had brought over a *Raki* and a plate of pickled sparrows which had been shot the week before in the vineyard behind the taverna. Sampson had learned to call them *Ampelopoulia*—the 'vineyard birds'. They were plucked while still warm from the kill. Some were roasted in the clay oven, situated out on the forecourt, till they were nearly black and then eaten. Others were popped into a jar of vinegar and wine and left for a week. The marinated delicacy tasted good but John had always wondered why anybody would take such trouble for such little meat. He sucked at the tender breast of the vineyard bird as he listened to Kokkos swearing, sending his companions at the night's card game to the devil.

"*Re tous keratathes,* they bloody well cleaned me out tonight with the Blackjack. Never trust a Cypriot at cards, John—yes even me—don't trust me!"

Much as he enjoyed Kokkos' company, John really had to concur with his host that, when it came to gambling, quite normal Cypriots could quickly change. Money did things to Cypriot folk. Although they were generous with strangers, for they possessed the *Philoxenia* of the ancient Greeks, when stakes were high, they couldn't trust themselves. They were, quite simply, natural gamblers. Kokkos clinked glasses with the botanist.

"*Iannis, re Koumbare,* tell me, I was in Tremithousa last night and they told me you were leaving Cyprus. Can this be true?"

"Oh, it's true alright, Kokkos."

"We'll all be sorry to see you go, Iannis. But I think you'll come back. They all do. This place gets a hold on people."

You're right there, thought John. So right. No place he had ever been had been quite as magical as Paphos. Even the country of his childhood in County Down, Northern Ireland, and the memories of farms and long summer days, playing in brooks and dreaming amongst the gorse bushes on top of the ancient Celtic forts, had not engraved such an affection in his mind as this Paphos region had.

It was already well after ten and John had things to do tomorrow. Kokkos was still calling out "*Cali nichta*" from the door of the Taverna as John rounded the bend which led up to the vineyards behind. The dogs barked, howling as though responding to some unearthly call within them. The clouds whipped past a moon which had just begun to wane. The *trizonia,* the crickets, had moved in to take up positions for night chorus, taking over from the cicadas who, having chirped throughout the day, had finally fallen quiet as darkness fell.

John had on his old black boots. They were his favourites, even though the left one was coming away at the seam where it joined the sole. They were comfortably part of him since, as John knew well, every Botanist, when working in the field, had a favourite pair of boots. Now, under the worn leather soles, the carobs crackled as he ascended the slopes of the hill. The twisted branches of the trees they had fallen from contorted in the light of the moon, as though many arms sought to envelop him. Carobs, John reflected as he walked, were what the Prodigal Son had given his pigs in the New Testament parable. The Levant and the Holy Land lay directly across the Mediterranean, about 35 miles away. Paphos had been where Paul and Barnabas had first exported Christianity and John mused that Paul must have appeared totally naive, appearing in the *agora* of Paphos to preach that God was a man and that his son had died, on a Roman cross, for mankind. He had taken a whipping for his pains. For the Paphites of the time, God was, most definitely, a woman, beautiful and sensuous.

John was now well up the small path and had come out of the vineyard into a grove, where he could smell the luscious deadly night-shade. He would lie here till first light and then continue his pilgrimage up to her altar at Kouklia. He reckoned to do the journey, in the cool of the morning, before the hot August sun came up.

He rolled out his thin beach mat in the thick grass, put his sleeping bag on top of it, placed the small rucksack at the head of it where it would function as a pillow, then removed his boots. He would keep the anorak on for protection from the cooler night breeze which, turning as it did at the top of the valley above him, would then descend, close to the earth till it reached the sea.

Now, stretched out in the grove, he allowed his thoughts to roam to the day's activities. Somewhere in the distance he could hear a lyre and drums and the muted sounds of feet dancing. It would be a wedding, probably. The music was evocative of ancient Cyprus—the instruments would not have changed much from thousands of years ago when pilgrims, getting off the boat, would have gathered in circles to keep each other company. Greek then, as now, was the language of their religion and culture. Silhouetted against the hillside but standing quite close to him was the Nightshade plant with its petunia—like white petals fluttering, its deadly belladonna berries teasing the stalk. Sampson realized that he had had slightly more cognaki and raki than he had planned for. His head swam a little. The music, the strong scent tickling the lining of his nose, the moon playing tricks with the light as it danced on the carob trees and the swaying flower stems, all contributed to the drowning of his senses. He could just remember how his morning had started—how he had packed ready for his final departure—the maps, the fossils he had collected, the specimens dried and stuck in tiny plastic bags—his diaries, his memories—stored away ready for the journey home. Then he struggled to remember the sea path he had taken, about midday, through the delicate forest that lined the Mediterranean and his arrival at the ancient port, the walk up though the modern town, the heat of the afternoon on his back as he had left dwellings behind and climbed towards Ieroskipos. The route of his pilgrimage faded as he tried to remember exactly how many cognacs he had taken to help sink the *sheftalia* sausages and the *ampelopoulia* in Kokkos' bar.

And then a flitting memory came to him. He was a schoolboy and it was English class. He was looking at a picture in a book of a temple, situated high above the sea, and the school master was praising Homer and the beautiful rhythm of his meter. Even much had been lost, the teacher explained, in translation but the lines were still beautiful in

English. Sampson felt the words struggling to come back to him. He had had to learn them by heart. Yes, Aphrodite was there in the very first line. Then they came to him and he said them out loud, there in the grove:

> "I will sing of stately Aphrodite
> Gold-crowned and beautiful
> Whose dominions is the walled cities of all sea-set Cyprus.
> There the moist breath of the Western wind wafted her over
> the waves of the loud-moaning sea."

He repeated 'moist breath' because he quite liked the sound of it. Then he slept.

The cockerels from the water-melon farms below ensured that he did not sleep later than six. He was up and immediately he set off, for he had eight miles to cover, and, in a very real sense, it was the most important day of his life. He had a rendez-vous with a Goddess. As he set out along the upper mountain track, the sea now to his right, he knew, not even in his wildest dreams, one year before, would he have seen himself giving even a passing thought to beings he considered to belong to mythology. These days, the compass of his world, physical and cerebral, made more allowance for what some might term the 'paranormal.'

His thoughts ran like a reflection on a personal development programme. 'Now that I'm actually going to meet her, it's an internal expurgation of the days when I wasn't truly alive and I know its physical ; my chest no longer tightens and the panic doesn't overcome me. The two-day-long migraines have gone. I've witnessed my own healing here this last year. She warned of her power and taught me how to really respect Cyprus and the beauty she protects here; taught me that this is not a place for western dreams and golf courses. It is an ancient, hallowed, place where the pace of life honours the dignity of man'.

By ten o'clock, the sun was high. His battered Panama kept direct light out but the sweat, where rim touched forehead, was beginning to make him feel uncomfortable. His pace, however, had been good and, having just passed Timi down on the coastal plain to the right, he knew he would soon be crossing the river Dhiarizos which tumbled down during the winter months out of the higher Troodos range to the sea. The river would now, in August, be almost dry.

Once over the river. he would follow a path near to the modern road that led out to Limassol for a few kilometres till he reached his goal, PalaeoPaphos (old Paphos), above which lay the ruins of Kouklia

It was just approaching midday when he walked into her circle. A temple—the greatest ever erected to her—had once stood on the spot, but now the only remains were the ruined pillars and they circled a great slab in the middle of the layout of ancient stones. He knew exactly where to go; had never been here but knew it instinctively. The sun immediately above was in sacrificial position. He approached quickly right up to the altar and, putting his hand into his rucksack, pulled out the little posy of wild flowers mixed with fennel leaves and thyme that he had collected from the dew-filled grove that morning.

Gently he laid his votive offering on her altar and addressed her.

"You know, I thought of you as some sort of savage being, jealous and vindictive. A beautiful lady died at the hand of her husband. Waves crashed in at Drepanum and nearly killed both Undiga and myself. You trapped the divers at Pomos too. Tell me. Why didn't you kill me and have done with it?"

He waited and he felt the stillness in the air. So hot and so still. Ancient times had witnessed just such a hush before the sacrificial knife came down. Of course, no answer came to John Sampson. He looked over to the right where a portrayal of her face was engraved. It could just be made out on one of the pillars. Her eyes were blind blobs of stone, expressing nothing, her sensuous mouth seemed to express rejoical in victory. A little puff of wind picked up the posie of flowers and scattered them over the surface of the broad altar. John thought that perhaps the answer would not be heard. It would, instead, be up to him to interpret one. There would be a game of symbolism and signs. Did the flowers mean anything? Was this the answer? Did his anxiety to identify and protect the rare species of the Akamas please her? Is that why she had not harmed him as she had the divers who'd been keen to illegally export treasures away from her island and to rob Cyprus of the symbol of its protector?

His second question spilled out.

"Were you jealous of Undiga?"

The enigmatic smile on the pillar was now half in shadow, as the sun retreated slightly from its position directly above. He found himself answering his own question again. Does she need to feel jealousy? No female has had so many thousands of years of worship or was ever so feared and revered. Why would she feel jealous of some mortal woman?

He walked around the altar so he could take in the breathtaking view of ancient pillars, lined against the blue of the sea which lay five hundred metres below. The last question had to come out.

"And where am I going next, now that you have changed me completely?"

Silence. A hawk in the sky circling, waiting for an unsuspecting animal to scurry out. Beyond it an aeroplane from Paphos Airport soared up and moved out over the Mediterranean Sea. That reminded him he was flying tonight and had to return to Paphos for another important engagement. He'd arranged to have dinner and a drink with Margo tonight. He had not had the chance to see her since her film team had returned with edited video material. She'd promised to show him what footage they'd assembled for Channel 4's 'Lost Treasures of Cyprus.'

He looked around and breathed in the tranquillity which this place offered. Reluctantly, he started off down the hill but had gone no more than ten paces when he paused. He had missed something; a final part of the ritual. Slowly and deliberately, he turned and shouted back in Greek, because only Greek would suffice . . .

"Kai Efharisto!!"

To offer thanks, he knew now, was the least he could do to the figure that had sometimes haunted him, sometimes brought him up on high, during his sabbatical year in Cyprus. Now he realized that she had healed him precisely by exposing him to the opposite elements of life. He hadn't felt really alive until he'd tangled with death. Beauty had not meant much without knowing what was truly ugly. His fear and insecurity had left him open to love. He knew he had been healed by a deep experience of the truths that Plato had advocated as the basis of all philosophy—namely that all states of nature and mind have opposites.

At six that evening, he drew up outside Margo's temporary flat, downtown in Kato Paphos. The film team had taken up six maisonettes in a block near the Cypria Maris Hotel, where the Director of the programme was staying.

Margo came out to meet him and greeted him warmly with a kiss and the familiar throaty Yorkshire twang which she liked to put on from time to time: "Eh, lad! How's things, then? You're lookin' a bit hot under the collar John! Had a long day, have you?"

After a light evening meal of salad with humus and eggplant, she showed him the highlights of what the team had done, whilst they shared a brandy sour. There were treasures from across the UN monitored border; beautiful Byzantine paintings and murals from the churches there. And then another episode had close ups of exhibits from the Nicosia and Paphos museums. There was the statue of Aphrodite he had first encountered at Pomos, looking now as though someone had sculpted her yesterday. Then the episode on the wildflowers. Sampson had to remark on the clarity of the colour and the beautiful shots which had caught great bunches of wild flowers in their natural setting. He knew his advice had been taken on that one.

"They'll luv this stuff back in Leeds," she had to remark. "Make a change from 'Gardening World,'" she chuckled. "And you'll be able to catch them on the telly in Oxford, John. I'm going to miss you, you know ; all that advice on where to go and who to meet! Cyprus is going to miss you! But this year has been successful for both of us. Look how many habitats of rare flowers you have identified and I've got some great pictures!"

Even as she spoke, he was reflecting on a kind of personal success but, on another level, something was still grating within him. His professional self inwardly nagged at him but he voiced his concern only to himself: "Not bad progress but where are the others? Where, for example, is that elusive *Epigogium Aphyllum*, the "Ghost Orchid' that has hardly been spotted for fifty years now in Cyprus? Maybe progress and the bulldozer have eradicated it."

Then Margo's voice brought him back. "John 'ave ya got a minute? I've got somethin' else to show you! That video we took at Tremithousa the first time we met—in the taverna—remember?"

"Have you kept that till now? Thought you might have erased the evidence by now." He secretly dreaded to see his old self; his shy approaches.

"You're joking! That's the best bit of video I took all year. Its just so authentic!" As she clipped in the DVD and pressed the remote, he turned away to the kitchen area, in a pretense of checking his passport and his ticket. He was out of sight but she had put up the volume and now she called him in to the living room.

"Get in here you! This is important footage for me. I thought I'd found a possible lover that night! Turned out I found a true friend and maybe it's better that way! Come on. That's right. Sit down there and watch the two of us at the Taverna! Oh I was a brazen hussy, weren't I? I actually chatted you up, do you remember?"

There, in the shadowy colours that night lights had reflected into the camera lens, were Akis and Soulla and the dishes laden with seasonal September vegetables and lots of oohs and ahs, as dish after dish of meze arrived on the table. Then there was a shot of him, hiding behind his hat, he imagined looking somewhat like a wounded animal. To his relief, the scene changed. There too were the people driving the old donkey down the street. The camera had turned on to the donkey's head,the flashes of red and white and other colours representing the flowers garlanded around the donkey's ears.

There were only seven minutes of film. He'd got up to go as soon as the video ended, for he had to get out to the airport. First on the last minute agenda was to return the jeep to Makris' agent in Kato Paphos. He'd only left himself an hour and a half before the flight would leave.

Something tugged at his sub-conscious memory but he could not think what it might be. He checked his wallet again; passport, ticket, money, receipt from Makris.

"Ah yes it must have been the receipt I was thinking of. I'll need that!"

Then, as he bent to kiss Margo on the cheek, he just as suddenly pulled away.

"Heh John! What's up then. Are you nervous or something? Five hours flight. Nothin to get worked up about and . . . ."

"Margo, that video! Can you run it back quickly and can you freeze the frame on the donkey's ears? Please quickly! I've only got a couple of minutes!"

"Ok! What's up exactly, John? You look like someone's shot an adrenalin injection into you!"

She found the place on the disk, went back to the food scenes and then allowed it to slow play for half a minute until they got to the ears.

"Hurry up, Margo! Please!"

She froze the frame. He stared with unbelief. He'd seen the white, he'd seen the blues and reds, he had seen all the varied colours in the flowers that night, nearly one year ago, but how had he managed to miss the star of them all? The fluted petals were a sensuous purple and ran, in a tell tale order, down the length of the long stem

Disbelief turned to surprise and surprise turned to a sort of shocked pleasure.

"Margo this means . . . You know what this means? I thought I was going to be lucky to spot our elusive friend the 'Ghost Orchid'. But this flower is even rarer. It has only been sighted in three locations since 1850 and belongs only to this Paphos region, where it has been very rarely spotted! This is the rarest of Cyprus endemic flowers, Margo. This is *Delphinium Caseyi*—we know it as 'Casey's Larkspur' Its absolutely unbelievable!

"You mean my lousy little video recorder just happened to be . . . ."

"It means everything, Margo. Margo, please, I'll have to take this to England. Its top of the list on the EU's Red endangered species list. Save a copy to the hard disk immediately. I'll make more copies in UK, when I get back to my botanical labs. You can have as many copies as you want but this record must not be lost to research! Then, I'll have to come back and find its location; speak to those people who picked it up over at the wine-press! That's what it means! It means worlds to me Margo. I simply can't believe it and . . . and here I am without any time left. Give me your copy for now, Margo. Give it to me and I'll get away. I'll see you very soon and anyway I'll call you from Bergen tomorrow or from London on Monday. OK?

'Well I never! Just imagine!

It took two minutes to copy to her hard disk. She slipped the CD into a small plastic cover and pressed it into his hands. At the bottom of her front door steps, they kissed and hugged each other in their excitement. Margo could only say:

"You did it. We did it. We caught a rare one!"

As John Sampson climbed into the jeep and set off in the direction of Makris garage, the video firmly placed in the side pocket of his overnight bag, he thought of the questions he had framed that day at the altar at Kouklia and wondered, in amazement, at the clarity of the answers he had received.

He would be on the plane tonight. It would not be long, however, before he would return to this island. He had made many friends here and had even lost some to the clutches of the final sleep. Moreover, he had to admit to himself, he had made one very important ally, one that would demand great respect and attention.

The Cypriot twilight was turning into night. One weathered marbled face would, by now, have been obscured in the dark shadows behind the altar at Kouklia.